Praise for The

“A dashing hero attempts a rescue but the maiden in this tower is no shrinking violet! Sparks fly in this entertaining tale of love, passion and adventure.” ***Christine Wells, bestselling author of* Sisters of the Resistance**

“I simply adored these two characters and their fairy tale romance.” **Gem of 2021 Award, *Kathy’s Review Corner***

"What a gorgeous story!! This beautiful tale was hot hot hot, with a love rich and grand. And seriously, can I please have my own stone tower... with a hot-blooded hero, a crackling fire and plenty of warm, comfy blankets while a storm rages outside?!” **5 stars, *GoodReads Review***

"If you're looking for a great Highland romance that mucks with your emotions and leaves you smiling like a loon, then I highly recommend giving *The Highlander's Rescued Maiden*." **5 stars, *Stacey is Sassy***

“This was a lovely way to end the series, one I’ve adored. From the Scottish settings, to the brawny Lairds and the high spirited women who married them, these stories have captured my imagination and catapulted me to mystical bygone eras. They put me in a happy place.” ***Jonetta, Blue Mood Café***

“Anna Campbell is a master at putting sizzle into sensual.” **5 stars, *Romance Book Haven***

"A riveting book from start to finish." **5 stars, *Tartan Book Reviews***

"*The Highlander's Rescued Maiden* has one of my absolute favorite meet cutes! I read it in just one night." ***Laurie Benson, Award-Winning Author***

"A joy to read!" **5 stars, *GoodReads Review***

"In this crazy world of a Global Pandemic or just everyday stresses, you can take a staycation and enter the world of Anna's love stories and hunky Highlanders. I highly recommend her books." ***The Reading Wench***

"I really enjoyed Will and Ellen's story! I loved watching these two fall in love." ***Historical Romance Lover***

"Yes! Yes! And yes! I absolutely love. Love. Love this book." **5 stars, *Amazon Review***

"One of the most beautiful love stories you will ever read. It's an emotional rollercoaster ride from start to finish." **5 stars, *Amazon Review***

"If 'forced proximity' romance is your catnip, you'll love this. It has a fairytale quality to it, that is just so enchanting." **5 stars, *Amazon Review***

ALSO BY ANNA CAMPBELL

Claiming the Courtesan

Untouched

Tempt the Devil

Captive of Sin

My Reckless Surrender

Midnight's Wild Passion

The Sons of Sin Series:

Seven Nights in a Rogue's Bed

Days of Rakes and Roses

A Rake's Midnight Kiss

What a Duke Dares

A Scoundrel by Moonlight

Three Proposals and a Scandal

The Dashing Widows Series:

The Seduction of Lord Stone

Tempting Mr. Townsend

Winning Lord West

Pursuing Lord Pascal

Charming Sir Charles

Catching Captain Nash

Lord Garson's Bride

The Lairds Most Likely Series:

The Laird's Willful Lass

The Laird's Christmas Kiss

The Highlander's Lost Lady

The Highlander's Defiant Captive

The Highlander's Christmas Quest

The Highlander's English Bride

The Highlander's Forbidden Mistress

The Highlander's Christmas Countess

The Highlander's Rescued Maiden

The Highlander's Christmas Lassie

A Scandal in Mayfair Series:

One Wicked Wish

Two Secret Sins

Three Times Tempted

Christmas Stories:

The Winter Wife

Her Christmas Earl

A Pirate for Christmas

Mistletoe and the Major

A Match Made in Mistletoe

The Christmas Stranger

His Christmas Cinderella (in the anthology A Grosvenor Square Christmas)

Other Books:

These Haunted Hearts

Stranded with the Scottish Earl

The Highlander's Rescued Maiden

The Lairds Most Likely Book 9

ANNA CAMPBELL

ISBN: 978-1-925980-17-2

Publisher's Note: This is a work of fiction. Names, characters, places, and incidents are a product of the author's imagination. Locales and public names are sometimes used for atmospheric purposes. Any resemblance to actual people, living or dead, or to businesses, companies, events, institutions, or locales is completely coincidental.

Cover Design: Hang Le

To my dear friend Judy Glen.

CHAPTER ONE

Isle of Bortha, Outer Hebrides, Scotland, August 1732

The wild wind that had blown Will Mackinnon's boat onto the rocky shore of this small island still whistled around his ears. Yesterday had been a perfect summer's day in the Hebrides, with the sky and water as blue as his mother's famously beautiful eyes. Today it was like the coldest corner of hell.

By God, he loved Scotland.

While the onshore gale persisted, there was no getting off this jagged speck in the Atlantic west of Lewis. Shivering in a wet shirt, Will set out to explore the place he'd call home, if only for tonight.

It didn't take him long. The island wasn't much more than a mountaintop in the ocean. He climbed the slope from the sandy beach where he'd pulled his boat, the *Leumadair*, up out of the roaring surf's reach, until he reached the summit. On his way, he passed a couple of tumbledown bothies but saw no sign of current inhabitants.

At the top, he looked west over an empty stretch of turbulent gray water. He could be the last man on earth.

His attention fixed on a ruined tower on a cliff, facing out across that heaving sea. These islands on Scotland's west coast were littered with fortifications, some left by the Vikings, some left by even earlier inhabitants. Curiosity lured him into a scramble down a scree-covered hillside to investigate.

The closer he got, the less like a ruin the tower appeared. It might even be substantial enough to offer the hope of shelter. He didn't fancy sleeping on his boat or in one of the ramshackle abandoned cottages with a roof open to the sky.

To his surprise, at the base of the tower, he found a stout oak door in excellent repair. Now that he stood next to it, the tower was taller than he'd expected, too. On this landward side, a line of narrow windows stretched up to the top. It perched on the edge of a promontory, so he couldn't see the side facing the ocean.

Once again, he glanced around. By heaven, this was a desolate spot to pass an afternoon. Like the tower at the end of the world.

Although the island seemed uninhabited, he knocked on the door. No response. He knocked again with a similar result.

A tug at the wrought-iron handle proved it was securely locked.

Will sighed and surveyed the structure with closer attention. The stonework looked rough enough to provide plenty of hand and footholds for someone who had grown up scrambling over the impressive mountains surrounding his father's castle at Achnasheen. He began to climb.

The stones were wet and slippery and at times, he was hanging by his fingertips. But he and his brother had conquered the mighty Cuillins on Skye, so he was used to finding purchase on an unpromising surface. His booted feet pressed down on protrusions mere inches in length, but big enough to allow him to make slow upward progress. At least the rain held off, although with every yard he ascended, the wind grew fiercer, whipping his long hair around his face and obscuring his sight.

The first window he reached was little wider than an arrow slit. Too small for a man built on his heroic lines to squeeze through. But Will saw enough through the opening to realize that inside, the tower was habitable. In the darkness, he made out the shapes of a couple of narrow beds and a few chairs and chests. If he could find a way in, this place would offer a fine refuge, as night descended, along with the rain he could smell on the blasting wind.

He was cold and wet and a dizzying three floors up before he came to a window wide enough to fit him. When he swung breathless over the sill, he set foot on something that felt like carpet. After the daylight outside, the sudden dimness within blinded him.

He sucked in a lungful of air, and his vision cleared to reveal a beautiful woman with golden hair glaring at him. She aimed a flintlock pistol straight at his heart.

Ellen saw the man's eyes widen as his hazel gaze focused on the gun, but he showed no other reaction. Certainly none of the cowering terror that she'd hoped to see.

"Och, lassie," he said in a velvety drawl that made every hair bristle. "This isnae much of a welcome."

"That's because you're no' welcome." Her hand didn't waver, and she responded with a coolness that almost matched his. Inside, she was a quaking mass of terror and rage, but she refused to betray any weakness to this brazen interloper. "I'd think that would be clear when I didnae open the door to you downstairs."

"It's a braw gusty day." The man rubbed his hands together to brush off the dirt from the climb. "I wondered if ye heard me over the weather."

"I heard ye all right. I'm no' at home to callers this afternoon." Caustic irony weighted the polite society phrase. "Now I'll thank ye to get out."

The devil made the perfect picture of male arrogance, standing there. Tall, unafraid, and breathtakingly handsome with his untidy mane of vivid auburn hair and his insolent expression. The wet shirt, grimy from his climb, clung to the hard muscles ridging his chest and abdomen. Even the bright red and black pattern of his kilt screamed masculine superiority.

Ellen had had quite enough of masculine superiority. This cocky intruder didn't impress her.

Or so at least she told herself.

"The way I came?" He tilted one mocking eyebrow and hitched up one hip with a nonchalance that he must know was risky in front of a loaded weapon. She supposed she should be grateful that he kept his distance. "Or will ye permit me to use the stairs?"

Her mouth tightened as she raised the gun. "I dinnae give a rat's behind, as long as you go."

A sardonic smile curled his lips. "In that case, I might choose the stairs. Or perhaps if ye put the gun down, I can introduce myself, and you can tell me who you are and we can converse like civilized beings."

The arrant coxcomb. He imagined sheer cheek might win out. Her tone remained implacable. "I dinnae want to converse with you. I want ye out of my tower. If you're wondering whether the gun is loaded and whether I ken how to use it, the answer to both those questions is yes."

"I'm sure it is, lassie." Humor lightened his eyes to sparkling green. "Ye have an air of competence that says you mean business."

"So I'll tell ye again." Her voice remained steady, belying the nerves that leaped about inside her stomach like excited puppies and made her feel queasy. "Get out."

"As ye wish, although I swear on my soul you're safe with me." He bowed, as if they were in a ballroom and not a rough stone tower on the remote edges of the kingdom. "Before I go, may I know the name of the lovely lassie who refuses me her hospitality on such a dreich day?"

His game-playing made her lips lengthen in irritation. "Ye know who I am."

He frowned as if he sifted his memory for a lady who fitted her description. She could already tell that the villain had a long list of women to count through. "Have we met before?"

"No," she snapped, annoyed at this masquerade.

His glance traveled over the round room, furnished with every comfort, and out through the large window behind her that faced the turbulent Atlantic. She saw the moment that shocked realization descended over his features.

This confident intruder was either a cursed good actor, or he really didn't know who she was. At least, he hadn't until now.

"By God, you're Fair Ellen of the Isles." His wonder sounded genuine.

"Ye expect a prize for guessing?" she asked sarcastically, still convinced he was pretending. While Bortha's isolation meant visitors were rare, enough would-be rescuers had turned up over the years for her to mistrust this one's claim of ignorance.

He didn't seem to hear her, but studied her with a bright-eyed interest that made her blush, mad as that was. "I've always thought ye were a myth, yet here you are. I've got a cousin who set out to find you about four years ago, all fired up to rescue ye from captivity. I told him he was a complete knucklehead and that he was chasing after shadows. Now it turns out that you're nae shadow."

"As ye see," she said stiffly, wondering in bewilderment how she was losing control of the discussion when she held the gun. Wondering why she was even having a discussion.

"As I see." He continued to inspect her as if she was about to sprout wings and fly off to Ireland. "The stories say that you're a prisoner. Yet I gather ye can leave the tower when you wish, if you had a choice whether to let me in or no'."

She was a prisoner, all right. "I have the run of the island."

"The rumors got one thing correct. I've never seen a woman so fair."

"Save your flattery." Her voice crackled with ice.

Compliments on her looks had stopped pleasing her, once she'd matured enough to realize that they disguised unspoken attempts to possess or control. Often enough, she'd cursed the face that she saw in the mirror. It hadn't done her any favors.

"Is your wrist no' getting sore?" He waved an elegant hand at the gun, as if it held no more importance than a toy. "By my faith, ye can put your pistol down. I mean you nae harm. I was looking for somewhere warm and dry to spend the night, and I thought the tower was empty."

Ellen didn't take up his invitation, although he was right – her wrist had started to ache. But despite his reassurances, fear pounded in her heart. Since she'd heard him try the door downstairs, she'd been clutching the gun.

She'd give this swaggering jackanapes one thing – he'd made quick work of scaling her tower, and he'd done it without ropes or assistance. At least...

A horrible thought struck her. "Are ye alone?"

That glittering curiosity made her feel like some sort of scientific specimen. "Aye."

Most of the men who reached the island in search of her had come alone, although one or two had arrived with armed backing. "And ye expect me to believe that you accidentally ended up on this rock in the middle of the sea?"

The man shrugged in response to her skepticism. "Whether ye believe me or no', that's the truth."

"So how did ye get here?"

"I took my wee boat out for a sail yesterday and got caught in the storm that sprang up. What is this island? It's no' on my charts."

"Bortha," she said, before she remembered that she didn't want to talk to her unwanted guest, she wanted him gone.

"And who is Laird of Bortha?"

"My father, the Laird of Inchgallen."

He frowned. “Inchgallen I know. I’ve seen it on my charts.”

She gestured toward a low, dark shape on the far horizon behind him. “That’s Inchgallen.”

The island she hadn’t set foot on in ten years. Just thinking about it was enough to make her heart keen in sorrow, despite the cruel treatment she’d received there. Inchgallen would always be home, the place she was born, the place where she belonged.

The man twisted to see where she pointed, before his attention returned to her. “If the stories about ye are true, the suitors for your hand were so numerous and so troublesome that your father locked you up in a tower to keep you safe.”

“It’s a fairy tale.” Scorn turned down her lips. “Does it no’ sound like a fairy tale to ye?”

He shrugged again. It seemed to be a characteristic response. “I told ye – until this moment, I’d never believed in the existence of the legendary Fair Ellen of the Isles, confined to her tower like a princess in a story.” He paused, surveying her with that intense attention that left her so rattled. She could already tell that a piercing intelligence accompanied his spectacular looks. “Yet here I am on a mysterious island with a girl in a tower, a girl with a face to make Helen of Troy green with envy. It makes me wonder if perhaps the rest of the legend is true.”

Contempt firmed the woman’s pretty pink lips. In the stories, Fair Ellen had been a sweet little cipher, waiting for a strong laddie to brave the tower’s defenses and climb to her rescue. Naturally in the legend, the grateful beauty would take one look at her savior and fall madly in love with him.

When his cousin Dougal had set out to free the imprisoned maiden, Will had told him that he had rocks in his head. Highlanders loved a great story. They cared much less whether the story was true. The tales of Fair Ellen were just another rumor, substantial as a wisp of sea fog.

As Will had predicted, Dougal hadn't discovered Fair Ellen, although he'd found true love on another small isle. Before Will was blown off course, he'd been on his way to visit Askaval, where Dougal and his wife Kirsty lived in wedded bliss.

Now it turned out that the wisp of sea fog that had intrigued Dougal held more than a kernel of truth. There was indeed a maiden in a tower on an island, although Will was delighted to find that the real woman had much more salt in her character than the gormless creature of rumor.

In the legend, Fair Ellen had been a mere slip of a girl. This was a grown woman in her mid-twenties.

As promised, she was beautiful, although he could see his compliments didn't please her. Nothing he'd done so far had pleased her. Yet for the life of him, he couldn't look away from her face.

Will came from a famously handsome family. His mother had been a famed beauty. But he'd never seen a lassie to rival Fair Ellen. Fair indeed. She looked like a Viking princess, which was no surprise, given that for centuries, Norse longships had sailed up and down this coast. Hair like moonlight. Skin like new cream. Eyes the pale blue of the sea at dawn on a fine summer's day. A delicate face with a pointed chin and a decisive jaw. A soft mouth that he'd give half his considerable fortune to see relax into a smile.

No smiles from Fair Ellen for Will Mackinnon. Hell's bells, she was holding him at gunpoint. He saw no reason to doubt her claim that she knew how to use the little silver pistol. That low, husky voice – damn it, even her voice was beautiful – had rung with confidence when she'd threatened him.

"Were ye no' listening?" Those spectacular ice-blue eyes narrowed on him. "I dinnae want to sit down and have a chat with ye. The only word I want to hear from ye is goodbye."

Amusement curled his lips. How he loved a challenge. The problem with most of the lassies he met was that they were far too eager to fall at his feet. The heir to Achnasheen was a catch, when he much preferred to play hunter than quarry.

Hoping that it would convey good intentions, he retreated to sit on the sill of the window he'd climbed through. Behind her, the view through the large window facing west revealed another squall sweeping in from the sea. "What if I want to stay? Will ye shoot me in cold blood?"

Another furious flash of those gorgeous eyes rewarded his impudence. The girl in the legend had always struck him as rather soppy and far too resigned to her fate to be worth the winning. The real Ellen offered a much more alluring proposition. Will had spent mere minutes in her company, and already he was sure that he'd like to know her better.

Of course, he wanted her, too. He doubted any man could behold those perfect features or that tall, slender body without feeling desire. But it wasn't just her appearance that stirred his masculine interest.

"If I have to," she said evenly.

Hoping he wasn't tempting fate, he spread his hands. "Go ahead, then."

A thorny silence fell, and he caught the first sign of uncertainty in her eyes as she surveyed him. "I don't want ye here."

"You'll like me when ye get to know me."

His effrontery didn't make her smile. "I don't want to get to know ye."

That was no doubt true. He was unused to girls who didn't giggle and twinkle and fiddle with their hair when he flirted with them. Ellen's flinty gaze told him that she was made of sterner stuff.

Will was perceptive enough to know that if she lived here alone, she must feel vulnerable. The pistol itself was evidence of that. He gentled his tone, as he hid a cold shiver. His shirt was wet and clammy. If she made him sleep outside tonight, he risked frostbite. Or drowning.

"I swear you're safe." He went on before she could argue. "The only shelter on this island is your tower, and I'm stranded here until the wind changes."

As if to confirm what he said, freezing rain spattered his back. It wasn't a downpour yet, but it promised to become one in the next few minutes.

"That's your problem."

He chanced another smile. It received the same frosty reception as his others. "Is there nae trace of Christian charity in your breast?"

Och, and what a comely breast it was. He didn't glance down to the curves filing out the modest blue bodice, but he'd already noted the generous bosom and slim but womanly figure. She wasn't voluptuous, but what there was of her was prime quality.

"No' for an uninvited intruder," she snapped.

"Perhaps for a sailor blown off course and requesting succor."

"I presume a sailor has a boat he can sleep on."

"It's only a wee vessel with no cabin."

"Then the sailor is likely to get wet."

He couldn't help it. She was so adamant against him, and it made for such a refreshing change. He burst into delighted laughter and rose, although he was careful to venture no closer. He didn't want to frighten her more than he had already. "You're a braw hard-hearted lassie, my lady."

His movement startled the girl into backing away, and Will's urge to laugh died an abrupt death. His first impression of physical perfection crumbled in an instant.

Fair Ellen was lame.

CHAPTER TWO

As Ellen stepped back, she swayed. Cursing himself for scaring her, Will ignored the gun waving in his direction and lunged forward. He caught her arm to save her from falling. "You're hurt."

"No," she said breathlessly, wrenching away. But he'd touched her long enough to feel her warmth and catch her fragrance. Lavender. Something fresh and feminine that made his skin tingle with sudden desire.

She cast a disgusted glance at the pistol and moved across to place it on the desk under the window. He watched her move, noting her uneven gait. His heart ached to see her limp. Something told him that when she'd denied any injury, it was no lie. Or at least the injury wasn't recent.

"Ye decided against shooting me?" he asked on an optimistic note.

She stared down at the gun with an unreadable expression on her exquisite face. "For the moment."

"I'd better watch my behavior," he said, desperate to see her smile.

No luck. She raised her head and subjected him to a hard look. He wondered how those eyes would sparkle if they lit with humor. "Aye, you'd better."

"And you're no' going to throw me out into the storm?" Outside the rain was coming down in sheets. If she banished him, he'd have a soggy time of it.

The corners of her lips deepened, but still no smile. "No' straightaway."

"Does that mean you'll let me sleep here?"

"It means I'm no' going to throw you out straightaway."

He closed the casement behind him to keep out the wet and gestured to two armchairs ranged in front of the blazing fire. "Would ye like to sit down?"

He should have noticed that the tower was inhabited before he started to climb. The wind must be blowing the smoke out to sea.

"Dinnae take over." As if he needed reminding that he was still on shaky ground with her, her glare was stony. "You remain in this tower very much on sufferance."

He smiled again. Again, she didn't respond. "Thank you."

Puzzlement made her frown. "For what?"

He swept one hand through the air. "For no' shooting me, for a start."

"Murdering my suitors always makes such a dreadful mess."

Caught unawares, he laughed. Then he realized that she wasn't laughing. He sobered and regarded her closely. "Ye don't mean that."

"Do I no'?" she asked in a neutral voice.

"May I introduce myself?" he asked, almost sure she was joking, but not quite ready to stake his life on the suspicion.

This was the strangest meeting. He'd never had an encounter like it. The bizarre truth was that Will was enjoying himself more than he could remember doing in years. He wished he could say the same for his companion, but to his relief, she no longer seemed frightened. The tense line of her shoulders had relaxed, although wariness lingered in her eyes.

"If ye wish. I doubt that you'll be here long enough for your name to matter much."

Ouch. "Nonetheless it will save ye from having to shout 'hey, you' when you want my attention."

That blue stare remained unrelenting. "I cannae imagine I'll want that either."

Will plowed on. In most cases, his nonsense had the lassies eating out of his hand. Something in him respected this girl for failing to fall for his tricks. He drew himself up to his full height and gave her another formal bow. "I'm William Mackinnon of Achnasheen."

When her lips tightened, he realized that she took his homage as a taunt. "I've never heard of it."

She set out to squash his pretensions. Unlucky for her, he had a good dose of his father's arrogance, so her prickly responses left him intrigued rather than chastened. "It's on the coast, looking over to Skye."

Ellen shrugged as if she didn't care. It was likely that she didn't, although every minute in her company made him itch to awaken her interest the way that she'd awoken his. His parents had a vibrant relationship, more fire than calm, cool water. He'd never found a lass ready to stand up to him, the way his mother stood up to his father. Odd to find her at last on a rugged rock in the wild Atlantic.

"That's well south and east of here."

"It is indeed."

He forced his attention away from the woman to take note of her setting and see what it revealed about her. So far, while he might have given the room a cursory glance, his attention had been all for Ellen.

The luxury surprised him. The tales of Fair Ellen had her languishing in a bare prison cell. But someone had furnished the tower like a palace. Expensive mahogany furniture in the first stare of style, silver-framed mirrors, and carpets from the East in rich colors.

She had plenty to keep her amused in her isolation, too. A clavichord and a harp. An embroidery frame. A small telescope. And books everywhere. Lined up on shelves. Piled high on the tables. Open on the desk with papers scattered about them. It reminded him of the study of an untidy Oxford don, if the don had a view of the ocean from his favorite chair.

Will's curiosity piqued. There was mystery here. Somebody had taken an enormous amount of time and trouble to ensure that the laird's daughter was comfortable. Yet she remained trapped and alone on a deserted island. From the moment, he'd climbed through the window, his instincts had told him that she was alone.

"Will ye tell me your name?" he asked, keeping his tone amiable.

It wouldn't take much to spook her back into aiming that gun at him. She was a long way from trusting him, and what concessions she made, she made with reluctance.

He couldn't blame her. Any stranger who came to Bortha came as a predator.

"Ye know who I am. Fair Ellen of the Isles." She spoke the name like an insult.

"So I may call ye Ellen?"

"You have already." Her tone dripped disapproval.

"In that case, ye may call me Will. All my friends do."

"I'm no' your friend," she said in a tone meant to discourage.

He smiled again. "No' yet anyway, Ellen."

Irritation weighted her sigh. "Ye may call me Miss Cameron."

He bowed again, not quite so deeply. "I'm very pleased to make your acquaintance, Miss Cameron."

She kept staring at him, as if he'd walked mud all over her carpets. Given the recent weather, he might have. He subjected his boots to a surreptitious inspection.

"I suppose you're hungry," she said with a notable lack of enthusiasm.

He shrugged. "A wee bit." In truth, he was famished. He'd eaten the last of the food that he'd brought with him this morning, while he'd wondered if he was about to find a watery grave. "Are ye offering to feed me?"

No trace of softening in his direction. Although he supposed if she meant to feed him, he'd advanced further in her estimation than he had when he squeezed through her window. It also spoke to her fear receding, thank goodness. "I'm about to prepare a meal for myself, and it's nae real trouble to cook for you, too."

"That's very kind of ye." And deuced unexpected.

She glanced with no special interest at the deluge outside. "No' really. I cannae send you out into that."

Will blessed the terrible weather, which hadn't been the case last night or when he'd washed up on the island. "It's an ill wind that blows nae good."

Yet again his attempt to raise a smile from her fell on stony ground. "Dinnae push your luck."

He gave her a smart salute. "As ye command."

She rolled her eyes, which made him laugh again. Which only gained him another flash from those disdainful eyes.

Ellen wondered what on earth she was doing, encouraging this handsome vagabond to stay. He was far too charming and far too aware that he was charming. Charming, but not, she thought, dangerous. Or in any case not violent.

She cast a quick glance at him under her lashes, noticing how proud and straight he stood in front of the window. Most lassies must go quite silly when he focused that sultry green-gold gaze on them. A sultry green-gold gaze that promised all sorts of forbidden pleasures.

Even she, who had learned in a hard school that men weren't to be trusted, couldn't dam the rush in her blood when that thin, expressive mouth curled in a lazy smile of appreciation.

He hadn't made a fuss when he noticed her limp, and he'd released her as quickly as he caught her when she lost her balance. Neither of those things gave her reason to assume that he meant her no harm. Yet she must be as silly as those other imaginary lassies. One touch of his strong, competent hands, and her asinine heart started performing cartwheels.

It was both disconcerting and unprecedented. A warning that she needed to send this cheerful young Adonis on his way.

Except that the weather made that impossible, and while she owed Mr. Mackinnon nothing, it seemed mean to force him out into the blustery downpour that filled her sanctuary with bleak gray light. She couldn't even see Inchgallen anymore, and the waves whipped up to foam at the foot of the rocks below her tower.

Ellen loathed displaying her physical infirmity before onlookers, but she couldn't stand around all day like a statue. Ostentatiously, so he knew she wasn't defenseless should he decide to pounce, she picked up the pistol and slid it into her pocket.

"Ye know you're in nae danger." For once, that deep voice held no trace of amusement.

She arched her eyebrows. "I know nae such thing."

"You have my word."

"Words are cheap."

"Mine aren't."

Odd that she believed him. As a rule, she wasn't inclined to rely on male promises.

But while she could picture Mr. Mackinnon seducing his way into what he wanted, he wouldn't employ force to gain his objectives. Good heavens, he wouldn't have to. Tall and strong in his kilt and with a face like a questing knight's, he just had to smile to get his own way.

That face remained serious, as his eyes locked with hers in silent affirmation of what he'd said. It was a remarkable face, all pure lines and planes, with an arrogant blade of a nose and a square jaw to save it from being too pretty.

When he wasn't smiling, he looked older. She realized with a start of surprise that he must be close to thirty.

Ellen made her way to the steps, wondering if he'd offer to help her. But Will Mackinnon got points there, too. He followed, but made no attempt to take her arm or question her ability to manage. From the first, she'd noticed how careful he was to keep his distance to avoid frightening her.

When they reached the kitchens on the floor below, she stoked up the fire and hung a pot of stew over it to heat up. She'd performed this task thousands of times, but she found herself fumbling and nearly dropping the spoon she used to stir their dinner. Her visitor's interest made her conscious of every move. She hated that she blushed with chagrin, just as she hated that he might think her in any way incompetent because of her bad leg.

Ellen waited for him to say something. If he expressed any pity, she might just pick up a cleaver. And who knew what mayhem that could lead to?

To his credit, he didn't mention her limp. She was so braced for a derogatory comment that it took her a moment to realize that he was moving around the kitchen, setting out plates and transferring the loaf of bread she'd baked that morning across to the table.

She turned to stir the stew again, amazed at his familiarity with household tasks. Amazed and unwillingly impressed. Her father wouldn't have lifted a finger to help.

She'd never heard of the Mackinnons of Achnasheen, but anyone meeting this man would recognize straightaway that here was no humble crofter's son. He carried himself with an easy assurance that spoke of wealth and breeding, even if she'd missed the significance of the heavy gold signet ring on the little finger of his left hand.

When she stepped away from the hearth, he glanced up with another smile. Devil take him, the rogue smiled a lot. "Is this all right?"

"Fine," she stammered.

"I assumed we'd eat down here. It saves carrying everything upstairs."

Her eyes narrowed on him, as she wondered if he referred to her ability to climb the steps, but he wasn't looking at her. Instead he was scanning the packed shelves. "Would ye like something to drink?"

"There's ale or wine. Or water." The island had a couple of reliable springs. If it hadn't, she couldn't have survived here. Then heaven only knew where her father might have stashed her. Probably on some rock halfway to Greenland.

"Wine?"

"If ye wish." Ellen wondered how she'd fallen into such easy domesticity with this interloper. Since her exile, a handful of men had come to her tower. She'd never invited one to share a meal. Good Lord above, none of them had made it through the door. Although she supposed in the strictest sense, neither had Mr. Mackinnon.

That had been quite a climb, further confirmation that he was agile and fit. His presence in her kitchen hinted that this particular trespasser posed a greater threat than any of his predecessors.

He shot her an ironic glance, as he turned to her with a bottle in one hand. "What did I say?"

Disoriented by the question, she blinked and tried to remind herself to stay on guard. The fact that he hadn't leaped on her yet didn't mean that he wouldn't leap on her later. Despite common sense telling her that if he meant to assault her, he could have done it upstairs once she'd put the gun down.

"What?"

"Och, you've gone as stiff as a poker again."

With a sigh, she let the tension seep from her body. "I'm no' used to entertaining gentlemen in my kitchen."

Or anywhere, in fact.

One of those intriguing smiles tugged at his lips. "I'm privileged in that case." He set the wine on the table and turned back to the dresser to locate something to open it.

"You make yourself at home, plague take ye."

He found a gun worm and opened the wine with more of that impressive competence. "Would ye rather run around and serve me?"

She bit back a bitter remark about running not being among her talents. He wasn't being snide or patronizing. She'd been on the receiving end of enough of both in her time to note the difference. "No."

"Good." He looked around again and shifted to fetch two glasses. "Nae wonder you're a wee bit nervy, stuck here all alone with nobody to protect you. I'm surprised you've managed to stay safe, in fact." The gaze he leveled on her was penetrating. "I assume...I hope ye stayed safe."

"Aye, I have," she said, before she remembered that her welfare was none of his business.

Her answer seemed to gratify him, as if he cared for her well-being. Which was crazy, when they'd only just met and she could be nothing to him but a curiosity.

"I'm glad." His voice hardened in a way that she'd never expected. Who would have thought? It turned out that he was more than a lighthearted flirt. "Just why the deuce are ye on your own and unprotected? It smacks of abominable negligence."

Ellen found herself answering before she recalled yet again that she wanted to keep him at a distance and send him on his way no wiser about Ellen Cameron and her life. "I dinnae live here alone. I have a maid, and my father supplies me with six men-at-arms who change every week."

Mr. Mackinnon surveyed the kitchen. "So where in Hades are they? If they were doing their duty, they should have seen me off when my boat struck the beach."

She spread her hands. "My maid had a toothache, so she went back to Inchgallen with the guards. Then the storm..."

His expression didn't ease. "I assume the guards are here to see that ye stay on the island, as much as to keep off unwanted intruders?"

Bitterness twisted her lips. He was quick, she gave him that. "I cannae sail the boat on my own. And I cannae swim to another island, even if there was one within reach."

Again she expected some remark about her limp, but his gaze remained on her face. "I have a boat."

"To steal me away?"

He didn't react to her sarcasm. "If ye wish."

A portentous silence crashed down. Ellen checked his features for signs that he was joking, but he looked grave as so far he seldom had.

While they'd put the meal together, she'd almost forgotten her fear. Now alarm woke to spread icy ripples down her backbone. She stepped back until her hips bumped into the bench, and she fumbled for the pistol weighing down her pocket.

"That wasnae a threat," he said in a quiet voice. Again, he kept his distance.

"Aye, it was," she said through stiff lips, as she closed a shaking hand over the butt of the gun.

Mr. Mackinnon leaned back against the dresser and folded his arms across his powerful chest. His air was casual, although he must know that she reached for her weapon. "I told ye you're safe, and I meant it."

"Ye just want to bundle me into your boat and carry me off."

Something in her hoped that he'd deny it, but that stare remained unwavering. "Aye, I want that."

She dragged the pistol up and aimed it at him. Her grip was woefully unsteady, but even if she was a quivering jelly, at this distance she couldn't miss. "Get out."

Mr. Mackinnon's relaxed posture didn't shift. Dear God, he didn't deign to glance at the gun. Plague take him, he was a cool devil. Ellen was caught between anger and admiration.

"You're no' going to shoot me."

"I'm perfectly capable of it," she said, wishing the response didn't emerge as a frightened squeak. She'd like to think that she was as proud and composed as a queen commanding her domain. But it turned out that she was just a scared little girl.

Those expressive dark auburn brows rose. "In theory, I know ye are. But you willnae put a bullet into an unarmed man who offers you nae resistance."

Curse him, she was sickly aware that he was right. She hated hurting things. She even hated wringing a hen's neck so that she could put it in the pot for dinner.

"Try me," she said, hoping he'd believe her, even if she didn't believe it herself.

"Ellen..."

"Miss Cameron!"

"Miss Cameron, I may want to carry ye away with me, but that doesn't mean you have nae say in the matter."

"Indeed it doesn't."

"If ye like, I'll take you back to Achnasheen and you can make plans from there."

"I'm sure I can," she said with more sarcasm. "It's no' as if I'm at your complete mercy, once you get me away."

For the first time since he'd offered to rescue her, the laughter lines around his eyes deepened. "Even if I intended the worst, my mother and father might have something to say about my depraved plans."

That sounded almost respectable. "Your mother and father?"

"Aye."

For a dazzling moment, freedom beckoned. These last ten years, she'd been a prisoner on this island, her world bounded by a dangerous sea that she couldn't cross. She'd managed to make a life for herself, even found a way to bring the outside world to Bortha. But the prospect of following her inclinations and going where she pleased was intoxicating.

And far too good to be true.

"But ye mean to woo me."

He shrugged, as if he saw no alternative to his decision. "I do."

"Because of my bonny face," she said in a sour tone.

The clever eyes that surveyed her seemed to discern her fear and her resistance – and every one of her shameful, secret longings, too. "I could look at ye for the rest of my life and count the years well spent."

She knew his words were idle flattery, although he sounded like he meant it. All the same, nothing stopped her heart from flipping over like a landed trout. "And if that's no' what I want?"

"Then we work out something else. I told ye, I don't intend to force you into doing anything you dinnae choose." He glanced around the kitchen with a speaking expression. "I can guess that you've already given up far too much dominion in your life."

That was true. It surprised her how much he'd seen in his short time here. "But you're saying ye want me?"

She braced for more coaxing, but he merely said, "Aye."

Then Ellen realized something else, and she let the gun droop as she regarded him in bafflement. "But you've seen me walk. Ye ken I'm lame."

CHAPTER THREE

Pity cramped Will's gut, pity that he knew he couldn't express. If he did, Fair Ellen was likely to shoot him. Already he could tell that she was a proud creature. He had enough pride of his own to understand hers.

So he kept his tone light as he responded. Nor did he straighten from his slouch against the dresser. "You speak about your lameness as if it places ye beyond redemption. It's a misfortune, no' a mortal sin."

Her lips firmed. "In the world's eyes, it does place me beyond redemption."

"Then the world is full of idiots."

"Including my father."

He frowned as so many things that had puzzled him about the woman's situation suddenly became clear. "Are ye saying your father exiled you to this island because you walk with a limp?"

"I'm saying he doesnae like damaged goods, in particular damaged goods thrust right under his nose." She spoke in a flat tone to hide how the rejection smarted, but instead, it revealed how the wound continued to bleed. "I'm a disgrace to the great clan of Cameron."

"Och, that's mad. What did your mother have to say about it?"

"My mother died giving birth to me. My leg was injured when the doctors tore me from her womb."

"I'm sorry."

"That I limp?"

"That ye lost your mother so young." He frowned. "Dinnae say they sent ye to this island as a baby?"

She shook her head, as to his relief, she set the gun aside on the bench. "No, my presence was tolerated on Inchgallen until I was fifteen, when my father remarried. My stepmother found my infirmity even more offensive than my father did, and she wanted me out of her sight. No' to mention that I look like my mother, and she didn't appreciate that at all. That's when the Bortha solution arose." Bitterness laced her words with acid.

Will couldn't blame her. He came from a loving family. The idea of his parents spurning him or any of his half dozen brothers and sisters because of a physical imperfection was unthinkable.

Except more went on here than just coldhearted cruelty. "When your stepmother wed your father, did she have daughters?"

"Aye. Two."

"Of marriageable age?"

"Twenty and twenty-one."

"She was clearing away the competition."

Ellen looked surprised. "But I limp."

"Aye, ye do." Will hated the way she'd accepted that her lameness made her unworthy. It was natural, he supposed, if she'd heard no other opinion while she grew up. "You're also the loveliest woman I've ever seen."

"Fair Ellen of the Isles."

The corrosive irony in her response scored his heart. "I doubt many men would care about any unevenness in your gait when you're so beautiful."

She didn't thank him for the compliment. He'd noticed that she seemed to hate her remarkable looks. "My father cared."

Aye, that was the difficulty, wasn't it? The first man with a duty to love and protect her had proven a hollow vessel. "Your father is a weak bastard."

Ellen released a shocked laugh. "You dinnae mind your words, do ye?"

Will shrugged. "Tell me I'm wrong."

The slump of her shoulders made him want to take her in his arms and offer comfort. When he'd first seen her, every masculine instinct had jumped to attention. But the attraction extended beyond a powerful male urge to possess a beautiful woman. He seemed to understand her heart in a way that he'd never experienced before.

It was mad to feel this affinity with a stranger. Yet somehow he did.

"No, you're no' wrong," she said in a defeated monotone. "So when I was fifteen, I was bundled away onto this rock, never to return to Inchgallen."

"And the legend of Fair Ellen of the Isles was born."

As he'd expected, that name made her lush lips twist in disgust. "Fair Ellen, who has one leg shorter than the other."

Will sent her a direct look. "You make too much of your infirmity. Ye seem to get around all right." She'd taken the stairs at a fair clip, and she'd had no trouble pottering around the kitchen.

"I refuse to be at anyone's mercy." Then a bleak expression shadowed her features. "Although in reality, I cannae stop my father from confining me here. I cannae get off the island. I cannae prevent presumptuous gentlemen from turning up to see what all the fuss is about. I cannae even send you on your way."

Will winced, as her weary rancor heightened his urge to comfort her. Comfort she'd no doubt reject as patronizing. "You're no' defenseless."

She straightened away from the bench and shot him a contemptuous look. "No, that I am no'."

It was a warning, he understood. He frowned as he considered her childhood. "Even if your father rejected you, there must have been people who cared about ye."

"My nurse loved me, and I had an aunt who protected me from the worst of it if she could. She died when I was ten. But my father is a gey godly man, ye ken. He saw my affliction as a curse from the devil – or a judgment from the Almighty on my unfitness to be his daughter. Most of the clan took their lead from him and steered clear of me. Or worse."

Will hid a flinch at the edge in her voice. "Did they hurt ye?"

"No' physically, apart from a bit of hair-pulling and a few pinches. I was the laird's daughter, nae matter how he despised me. But there were always spiteful whispers, just loud enough for me to hear. It was almost a relief when I first came to Bortha."

Will's heart clenched in sorrow and futile rage so strong that it tasted like rust on his tongue. This beautiful woman had been an outcast among the people who should have loved her most. How the insults and ostracism must have stung her proud spirit.

"The legend talks about suitors." Fifteen was early for a lass to wed, but not unheard of. And Will couldn't be the only man who had found her appealing, weak leg or no.

"Aye, a few men asked for my hand, although they became fewer once they realized I couldnae walk straight. But my father was convinced that if the Good Lord meant me to wed, he'd have made me whole. What a disaster if the disgrace of my infirmity infected the next generation, and word spread of bad blood in the Camerons."

"But ye said that it was inept doctoring that injured your leg."

"Who can be sure it wasnae divine providence? At times, when life became unendurable on Inchgallen, I lent some credence to my father's idea of a curse. I suppose I was lucky nobody called me a witch."

The word and the threat it implied turned Will's blood to ice. He was a modern, educated man who lived by rational principles, but not everyone in Scotland was so enlightened. Only five years ago, some poor old woman in Dornoch had been burned alive for consorting with the Devil. "Ye were in danger."

"Aye. Inchgallen is an old-fashioned place. Better Bortha than a fiery death."

"Better a father who stood by his daughter and had the good sense to see that she was the victim of bad luck rather than supernatural forces."

"Aye, well, while what you say might be true, that father is no' Big Jock Cameron of Inchgallen." The tired certainty in her voice made Will want to punch something. Preferably Big Jock Cameron's no doubt self-satisfied face.

He'd never met the Laird of Inchgallen, but he'd known men like him. Superstitious. Bigoted. Convinced that they had a special right to the

Creator's attention. Minds sealed against anything that didn't fit their view of the world.

Ellen turned away to stir the stew that bubbled on the fire. She used a couple of dishcloths to lift the pot and carry it across to the table.

Will's hands closed at his sides as they itched to take the pot from her. He already knew enough to see that she'd interpret an offer of help as an expression of pity. Whereas this strong woman sparked his admiration. She had a stalwart, independent spirit.

By heaven, if she hadn't, her childhood and these years of captivity since would have crushed the life out of her.

"Sit down and eat," she said, dishing stew onto the fine porcelain plates that he'd set out. "It's my father's venison. He doesnae stint, when it comes to luxuries."

That was one way to quiet a guilty conscience. The Laird of Inchgallen must recognize that he'd done the wrong thing by his daughter, even if he didn't want to admit it.

"I noticed the books and musical instruments upstairs." Will sat at the table while Ellen carefully placed the pot on an iron trivet in front of the fire. The warm kitchen meant that his shirt was nearly dry, although he wished he had something clean to wear.

"Aye, my jail cell is furnished with every comfort."

No wonder she felt resentful. Life had dealt her a very poor hand indeed.

He reached across to cut a couple of slices of bread. His mouth was watering. She'd served up a savory feast that smelled like heaven to a man who hadn't had a hot meal through a hard, cold day. "How long have ye been here?"

She took some of the bread and buttered it as he began to eat. The food was delicious. Although he imagined that to Fair Ellen, it must taste like prisoners' rations. "Ten years."

So she was twenty-five, three years younger than he was. He wasn't surprised. The moment he'd seen her, he'd recognized that this was no innocent child, but a mature woman. A mature woman who had spent a decade confined on this barren rock. The idea hardly bore thinking about. He hid renewed outrage at her father's unconscionable treatment of her.

Will poured their wine and raised his glass to her. "Thank ye for taking pity on a storm-tossed traveler."

Her eyes narrowed. "A gey canny one. I'm still no' sure how ye managed to inveigle your way into a meal and an offer of a bed for the night."

"What can I say? We Mackinnons get what we want, one way or another."

When his careless answer left her looking troubled, he cursed his impulsive tongue. "You certainly managed to get more of my story out of me than I meant to share. How the deuce did ye do that?"

He sipped his wine. Its quality was no surprise. Another sop to her father's conscience. "Cunning and determination?"

To his surprise, a brief laugh escaped her. "Effrontery and damn-your-hide impudence, more like."

He smiled back, even as his wayward heart crashed hard against his ribs. Ellen Cameron was breathtaking when she was proud and cold and determined to protect herself from assault or curiosity. But that couldn't compete with how winsome she became when she smiled.

Will struggled to clear his swimming head, as he swore on his life that he'd make sure she had plenty to smile about from now on. He wasn't by nature a knight in shining armor like his cousin Dougal, all puffed up on old legends. But when he pledged himself to Fair Ellen now, no knight of old could have made a more sincere vow.

This was a decisive moment in an existence that had for the most part been plain sailing. But he wasn't about to share his thoughts and lower the mood between them. Not now when he'd got her to laugh at last.

As he returned his attention to his dinner, he kept his tone easy. "That, too. It's in the blood. My father kidnapped my mother, ye ken."

Her eyes widened with alarm. "Dinnae forget I'm armed."

Damn him, he grew too confident, although he noticed that she'd relaxed to a point where she needed to look around to see where she'd left the pistol. "How could I forget?"

Ellen stood and slid the gun into her pocket. "You're here because of the weather."

He was here because of much more. At least he was, now that he'd discovered the treasure concealed on this unpromising island. "I appreciate the hospitality."

Her brief amusement had died, blast it to hell. He wanted her to smile at him again. He wanted that with an urgency that bewildered him.

"Once the storm passes, you're on your way."

Will set down his knife and fork and studied her. "Ye don't want to come with me?"

As Ellen resumed her seat, her lips curved downward. "And exchange one prison for another?"

He spoke seriously. "Ye need to trust me."

She pushed away her half-empty plate. "No, I don't."

"I give ye my word that I have your best interests at heart."

This time, her laugh was grim. "I find that hard to believe. After all, you're a man."

Anyone would be cynical after what she'd been through. He couldn't even blame her for doubting his honor, now that he'd told her that he wanted her.

With a sigh, he went back to eating his dinner and pretending that her gaze on him didn't feel like a physical touch.

"Nae argument?" she asked after a bristling silence.

He took another sip of his wine. "Do ye want one?"

"So I cannae trust you?"

He shrugged. "You know I'm no' going to jump on ye. If you didn't know that, storm or nae storm, you'd pitch me out on my ear. As far as trusting me beyond the immediate moment, ye just need to get to know me better."

"More effrontery."

"If you like." He set down his glass. "Would ye care to hear the tale of how my father wooed my mother?"

"He sounds as impudent as his son."

"Och, he's much worse."

To his satisfaction, the corners of her lips deepened, as she fought not to smile. "We're stuck here for the moment. Ye may as well provide some entertainment in exchange for the inconvenience."

"Sing for my supper?"

"Aye."

Only as Will lay down on a guard's bed in the room below the kitchen did he put a name to what had filled Fair Ellen's eyes as he told her about Achnasheen and the doughty Mackinnon warriors who ruled it. It was longing. Longing for easy social contact with her equals. Longing for a glimpse of a world beyond the narrow confines of Bortha. Even more, longing for a friend.

Will could be that friend.

If she let him, he could be so much more.

As he folded his arms under his head and stared up at the heavy beams crossing the ceiling, he swore that she'd never be lonely again.

Wooing Fair Ellen wouldn't be easy, but by all that was holy, William Drummond Mackinnon was the one man in creation equal to the challenge.

CHAPTER FOUR

Ellen woke the next morning in her bedroom at the top of the tower and listened to the wind howling around her eyrie. The gale sounded even worse than yesterday. There would be no sailing today.

As she snuggled down under the blankets, she found herself smiling in forbidden pleasure.

Then her smile faded as disquiet flooded her. Dear Lord, she must have rocks in her head.

Sightlessly she stared at the tapestry of the Judgment of Paris that hung on the wall opposite her bed. She'd spent the last ten years sending the few suitors who found their way to Bortha to perdition. Or to be more accurate, her father's men-at-arms had. Whenever a stranger landed, she stayed out of sight. Far better that anyone who came was never sure that they'd found Fair Ellen's tower.

Yesterday, when the far too confident for his own good William Mackinnon had had the temerity to invade her stronghold, he'd been just another man out to claim a woman, no matter what the woman might prefer.

Except right from the first, Mr. Mackinnon hadn't been like those other men who had come to Bortha in search of glory and a bonny bride to carry away as a prize. He'd said that he found her island by accident, and she was now inclined to believe him. Nor had he treated her as an object, but as a person. He understood so much about her life. At times, too much for her peace of mind.

She was well aware that he'd had a hundred opportunities to overpower her and have his way. For pity's sake, last night, she'd set the gun down on the table when its weight in her pocket annoyed her. The weapon sat there for the rest of the evening, mere inches from his capable hand. He hadn't even glanced at it.

No, instead, his eyes had been all for her. Eating her up with a concentrated attention that had her heart performing acrobatics in her virginal breast.

Those eyes made a claim on her. A claim just as greedy as any made by the idiots who turned up, believing a serenade was enough to win her favor. Or those who arrived with a rougher wooing in mind.

Any suitor soon saw the wisdom of abandoning his quest when he met half a dozen stoutly armed guards.

Yesterday she'd told Mr. Mackinnon that she was interested neither in rescue nor in him.

Both those statements were lies.

With a groan, she tugged the covers over her head. What on earth was wrong with her? The heir to Achnasheen was a man. Why should she imagine that he was any better than the rest of his selfish, careless sex?

Except that he'd been kind about her limp. No, he'd been better than kind. He'd noticed it, but it hadn't seemed to matter. None of her unwelcome swains had come close enough to discover the flaw that shattered the myth of Fair Ellen of the Isles. William Mackinnon had, yet her infirmity made no difference to him at all.

He hadn't hovered at her elbow to give her help she didn't want. He hadn't pretended to ignore her limp. He'd somehow seen it as an essential part of her, the way nobody else ever had.

It could be a trick. But to what purpose? There was nothing to stop him seizing her. Instead he talked to her, and her lonely soul blossomed like a dying plant given water.

She was fond of Susie, her maid, and she had her correspondents, and the guards had become familiar companions over the years. But it wasn't enough. She hungered for intelligent conversation, for an equal, for a friend.

One night did not a boon companion make. But one night of urbane conversation with an interesting man proved a harrowing reminder of her isolation.

Through the years, she'd settled into a routine of full days that left no time for brooding over her travails. Last night, all that hard-won acceptance had disintegrated under a handsome man's smile.

However the world wittered on about Fair Ellen of the Isles, she was too aware of her physical imperfection to feel beautiful. Her father's lifelong disgust was eloquent testimony to how she failed to measure up. But William Mackinnon regarded her with a wholehearted approval that made her feel fully human.

Ellen couldn't resist admiring him, too. And not just for his conversation. She wanted to run her hands through that mane of rich red hair and cuddle up to that strong, vigorous body. She wanted him to put his powerful arms around her and keep her safe. She wanted him to press that smiling mouth to hers.

Despite the suitors who came to her door, she'd lived a life devoid of desire. Last night, she'd learned how desire could burgeon, irresistible and without warning.

Her imprisonment was a terrible thing. Suffocating and lonely and stultifying. Yet while her tower might constrain her, it also kept the world away. The world offered untold excitements, but it also represented danger. Danger she sensed with every cell in her body when she gazed with covetous pleasure on a good-looking young man with the devil in his eyes.

Ellen remained troubled and confused when she came down to her study, one floor down from the bedroom. She discovered her disturbing intruder lounging on the window seat, looking out over the mountainous seas. His smile added a sunlight that the weather lacked.

"Good morning, Miss Cameron," he said, rising and bowing. "What a bonny sight you make on a dreich day."

With a nervous gesture, she touched her hair. Mostly she dressed for practicality. Today, she'd dithered over her hair, until she'd told herself she was a silly goose and bundled it up in a loose mass of curls. A more elaborate style than usual. More elaborate and more flattering.

She'd also taken longer over choosing her gown. Instead of yesterday's plain blue dress, she'd chosen a cream chintz *robe à l'anglaise*, embroidered with peonies and peacocks. Ellen loathed to think that she preened for her visitor, but once she'd put on the pretty gown, she couldn't summon the will to change it again. Although given that she had to prepare their meals and look after the livestock, this was a cursed stupid frock to wear.

"Thank ye." She struggled to steady her voice to hide the way her heart leaped around like a grasshopper. But excitement quivered under her words, and she suspected Mr. Mackinnon heard it.

He wore the same clothes, the striking red tartan a vivid splash of color against the gray light. Auburn bristles marked his cheeks and jaw. The incipient beard increased his piratical attraction. "The weather is worse."

He was back to eating her up with his eyes, as if he couldn't get enough of the sight. That intense stare did nothing to calm her heart's daft antics.

"Aye, I know," she said, cringing at the bright tone that betrayed how the bad weather suited her.

Ellen might be glad that Mr. Mackinnon was caught on the island, but she wasn't sure she wanted him to know that. She laced her fingers together at her waist and tried to contain the giddy anticipation bubbling in her blood.

"I'm afraid we're stuck here together, at least for today," he said.

"I'm sorry."

He looked startled. "Are ye?"

Blood rushed to her cheeks. She hated feeling so awkward. Men from all over the Highlands might dream of pursuing her, but she was woefully inexperienced in how to attract one particular laddie's interest. "No' at all," she stammered.

When that flashing smile appeared, her heart set off on another breathtaking whirl.

"I'm delighted to hear that. Are ye still armed?"

"Oh..."

His smile intensified. "I'm glad you're no'."

"It's...it's upstairs."

"That's where ye sleep?"

"Aye." She shifted from one foot to the other, while she couldn't help thinking about inviting him upstairs into the beautiful bed with its carved dolphins and mermaids. With a speed that left her dizzy, her interest in this engaging stranger had turned carnal. She enjoyed his company, but it wasn't enough to satisfy her yearning. Every minute strengthened her wicked curiosity to feel the touch of those elegant hands.

She struggled to remind herself that she'd only met this man yesterday. Although somewhere between threatening to shoot him and this morning's blushing pleasure in his presence, she'd accepted that he meant her no harm. On a physical level, at least.

Mr. Mackinnon gestured to the walls of books and the chaotic desk. "Ye seem to have all the latest novels and periodicals."

"Aye."

His smile developed a disconcerting tinge of tenderness that made the breath jam in her lungs. "Och, you're very agreeable this morning."

She found herself smiling back, as she subsided into her favorite chair beside the fire. "I'm feeling a wee bit jittery. I told ye that I'm unused to entertaining gentlemen. I'm unused to company at all."

"You're no' still afraid of me?"

She bit her lip and cast him a questioning glance under her eyelashes. "Should I be?"

"I willnae do anything ye don't want me to."

That was just what she was afraid of. "Have ye been up long?"

"About an hour."

It was still early. For once, she had an exciting alternative to her daily routine, so she hadn't wanted to linger in bed. "Have ye eaten?"

"I was waiting for ye."

Ridiculous for that answer to warm her heart. It didn't mean anything special. This man had excellent manners, if one overlooked his habit of climbing towers and breaking in where he wasn't invited.

Ellen stood to go downstairs and start breakfast, but he waved at her to stay in the chair. She noticed that he'd fed the fire. The room was a cozy refuge. "Breakfast can wait a moment or two. Tell me what ye do in here."

"Why?" She cursed the nerves that made her sound ungracious.

His smile hinted that he didn't mind the sudden sharpness. That was something she'd noticed yesterday. He seemed to appreciate a woman with a bit of sauce in her.

When Ellen disagreed or questioned him, he responded as if talking to someone with a brain met with his approval. From his stories, she'd discovered that the Mackinnon women were powerful figures, starting with his mother Bonny Mhairi.

He relaxed back on the window seat. Perhaps because she was so conscious of her physical awkwardness, she'd always been powerfully aware of the way other people moved. Will Mackinnon had the grace of a dancer. Wherever he landed, he created an appealing picture. Lazing against her window onto the Atlantic, he was as loose-limbed as a cat.

"Because I'm interested." Mr. Mackinnon shot her one of those crooked smiles that set her pulses rushing. "No' to mention we'll be inside all day.

Perhaps tomorrow, too. We need something to talk about – unless you'd prefer to play cards."

"I have nothing to wager."

His comprehensive inspection of her person stirred wanton heat. "I wouldnae say that."

Her blush was back. Good heavens, it was too early in the day to get all hot and bothered. "Mr. Mackinnon..."

He gave a short laugh, and the deep, velvety sound made every hair on her body stand up and pay attention. "I'll stop teasing ye."

What was this sorcery? She'd spent twenty-five years thinking of her body as a mere means of getting around, and not a terribly efficient means at that. After less than a day with Will Mackinnon, she felt like she was on fire.

"Save it until you've had your porridge, at any rate," she retorted and basked in the appreciation gleaming in his eyes.

"How do ye fill your days? I'm guessing you dinnae sit here, staring out to sea and praying for some gallant adventurer to rescue you."

Her snort expressed disdain. "How asinine, to sail to the edge of the Hebrides in search of a lady who may no' even exist. If ye do happen to find her, you know nothing about her. She could be stupid. Or a shrew."

And all of these fantasy Ellens were lame.

Mr. Mackinnon shrugged. "Men can be asinine. Even I've done the occasional stupid thing, and I'm a paragon of the sex."

She burst out laughing. He'd made her laugh last night, too. "I'm sure."

"So tell me about your life."

For years, nobody had been interested in her. Her longing heart opened wider to him, even as native caution warned her to be careful. It would be too easy to fall under Will Mackinnon's spell.

"I write about Highland folklore. My nurse on Inchgallen was a repository of the old stories and the old ways, and I'm putting together a book of some of the tales she told me when I was growing up. I correspond with scholars all over Britain, too."

"Well, I'll be damned." More of that sinfully addictive admiration lit his face.

"I have a lot of hours to fill," she said, unable to mask her regret at that reality.

"And your father doesnae mind?"

"I promised him I'd make nae reference to my circumstances or the fact that I'm a woman. Everything comes to me via Inchgallen. He used to check my letters, but these days, he cannae be bothered. The men-at-arms bring the post each week when they change shifts. I sign everything E.C. Cameron. That's how I'm published."

"You're published?"

"Aye. In a few antiquarian journals."

"I take my hat off to ye."

"Thank you."

He looked thoughtful. "So Fair Ellen isnae quite as cut off as I'd thought. Although she herself could be a heroine in one of those Highland tales."

"It's mad, is it no'?" She sliced a hand through the air to indicate the irony. "I'm a prisoner, yet my mind can roam where it wants."

She liked her anonymity when she wrote as E.C. Cameron. Fair Ellen was a powerless pawn, whereas the scholarly world treated E.C. Cameron as an equal.

Mr. Mackinnon's hazel eyes were somber and disturbingly perceptive. "But ye remain a captive."

She heaved a weighty sigh, and her spurt of uncharacteristic self-satisfaction vanished. "Aye, I remain a captive."

A heavy silence fell. He shifted his attention to the sea outside. Stark, gray light illuminated his commanding profile. If Ellen played the heroine in an old tale, Will Mackinnon looked like the perfect knight to save her. Avid eyes traced that straight nose and square jaw, and the way his abundant red hair sprang back from his high forehead.

But he was more than handsome. The mind behind those chiseled features was sharp, and those glinting eyes saw too much.

Had they noted her penchant for him? She had a sick suspicion that they had. She wondered if she'd been unwise to leave her gun upstairs, even as she recognized that the moment when she might have shot him had passed. If it had ever existed at all.

He turned to her with one of those quicksilver smiles that lit his face to a male beauty that sent her heart somersaulting. "Perhaps after breakfast, you'll show me your work."

"I'd like that," she said, proud of her steady tone. Even as her witless heart yearned toward him and begged for him to admire her.

CHAPTER FIVE

Will studied his lovely companion in the candlelight. They shared the window seat in the study, the place he'd realized was the heart of this rugged tower. The room with the books and the musical instruments, and the desk where she wove the astonishing creations of her mind. The remains of their dinner littered a small table, and they were finishing the fine hock he'd chosen to accompany the chicken and ham pie.

Well was this lassie called Fair Ellen. He'd spent the day conscious of her beauty in a way he couldn't remember experiencing before. By now, he'd reached a point where he hardly noticed the limp that had seemed such a tragic misfortune when he'd first seen it.

She'd been so self-conscious about her lameness, but as the hours together passed, she became easier in his presence. He liked that. When she abandoned her wariness, she was charming company, interesting, clever, curious. It was a shock to realize that this day trapped on a rock in a roaring sea was one of the most pleasant he could remember.

And in contrast to Ellen's, his life had been full of agreeable experiences.

"I think the storm will continue tomorrow, too," she said, staring into the murky darkness. He suspected that she spent a lot of time sitting here, looking out across the sea that she could never cross.

"That wind might even be stronger than it was." He'd become accustomed to the raging gale and the ocean pounding at the foot of the cliff. The Isle of Skye sheltered Achnasheen from the worst of the weather, so this fierce wind from the Atlantic left him awed.

And grateful.

The tower was stout and well-built. Not a breath of a draft squeaked through the stones to disturb the firelit warmth. But it would be impossible to venture out on his boat tomorrow. Nor would Ellen's jailers be able to make landfall.

For at least one more day, this woman was his.

She must share the same thought. That had happened several times today. Will would find her voicing a notion that crossed his mind, as if taking up a conversation they were already having. "You're stuck here."

He smiled. "I couldnae be marooned with anyone more charming."

Her glance was unimpressed, although he'd been sincere. He thought back to what he'd heard of her, not least from his muddleheaded cousin. The girl in the legend had sounded like a brainless doll. The real Ellen had considerably more backbone, and a sardonic sense of humor that he appreciated. She was devilish pretty, but more than that, she was intriguing.

"Let's see if ye feel like that after a week."

It might be insane, but at this moment, the idea of a lifetime cooped up with Fair Ellen of the Isles sounded like an invitation to paradise. "Is that the longest a storm has lasted?"

Looking pensive, she sipped her wine. "Christmas two years ago, nobody could get a boat off the island for a month."

He rubbed his hand over his newly smooth chin. Earlier, he'd unlocked that stout door and gone outside to retrieve some of his belongings from the *Leumadair*, including his shaving tackle and a clean shirt. He'd also taken the opportunity to pull the craft higher up the beach and under an overhanging lip of rock. "Were ye on your own then?"

"No, Susie and the men-at-arms were trapped, too."

"Did ye run out of food?"

Her quick smile made his heart jump and jerk like a salmon on a line. In repose, her face was as pure as a marble angel's. When something caught her attention, her expression awoke to sparkling life. "Are ye afraid you might starve?"

"We can always eat Buttercup."

Ellen gave a horrified laugh. "Poor Buttercup."

Buttercup was the milk cow in the byre behind the hill. He and Ellen had twice braved the weather to tend her. They'd also fed the hens providing the tower with fresh eggs. Will's first quick reconnoiter of the isle had missed the sheltered hollow containing the livestock.

"There's nothing left on the boat. Even if I hadn't eaten it already, the food I packed for my day's sailing wouldnae quite meet the standard of tonight's dinner."

"Never fear. There's plenty to eat, although we might end up living on scones and potatoes, if this wind goes on too long."

"Buttercup is safe?"

"Aye, she is."

A silence fell, surprisingly companionable, given how he ached to kiss his glorious companion.

"I admire ye," he murmured after a while. He reached forward to place his empty wineglass on a mahogany table, then rested the back of his head against the window. Behind him, the wind whistled with a ferocity that should worry him, except that right now he hoped it blew until doomsday. "You've turned adversity into a kind of Eden."

As she stared into her wine, her lips curved down. She'd partaken more sparingly than he had. "It's a lonely Eden."

He was damned sure that it was. "Were ye never tempted to throw yourself into a suitor's arms? If only for a change of scenery."

Her hissed exhalation conveyed her poor opinion of that idea. "No."

Will studied her, desperate to understand what went on in her head. Her circumstances were unusual. Hell, they were so unusual, he found it hard to get his mind around her bastard of a father's medieval solution to his daughter's infirmity.

But aside from her bizarre circumstances, she was an unusual woman. And one of exceptional courage. He tried to imagine mustering the mental fortitude to endure ten years' imprisonment here. He wouldn't have borne Ellen's travails with nearly her spirit.

"Ye could have left Bortha and found the things that give most women joy. A husband. Children. Friends. A chance to run a home."

"A man to push me around. A family to be disappointed or embarrassed that I'm no' perfect. A crowd of people to point and whisper about curses from the devil. I've already suffered that, in my father's house."

Ah, the limp. Will might have come to disregard it, but the wound that her father had inflicted when he'd repudiated her continued to suppurate. "They cannae all have been scoundrels, the suitors."

Her stare burned. "I suspect any who werenae scoundrels were idiots."

A brief laugh escaped him. "Which category do I fall into?"

The sharp intelligence behind her inspection made him squirm. All day, he'd resisted mentioning his desire, because he wanted her to trust him. But they both knew that if she gave him the slightest encouragement, the fragile barriers of propriety would dissolve.

"You're no' an idiot."

He gave a grunt of appreciative amusement. "So I'm a scoundrel?"

Those ice-blue eyes continued to delve into his soul. "Are ye?"

"Nae more than most men," he said lightly. His voice lowered into seriousness. "Do you no' want a husband and children? Love?"

The last word hung in the air as if written in letters of fire.

Ellen frowned as she stood. "What the suitors offer isnae love."

"That doesnae mean it could never become love."

"Even if I was tempted, ye forget my father has stationed men-at-arms to guard me. They're no' here just to keep foxes out of the henhouse. They're here to make sure the hen stays in the coop."

"No man-at-arms ever expressed an interest in ye?"

Her gesture was dismissive. "They ken the truth about Fair Ellen of the Isles."

His lips compressed. How he wished her dolt of a father was here so that Will could give him a good kicking. What harm his callous rejection of this lovely girl had done. "That she limps?"

He caught a flicker of what looked like shame in her eyes. "Aye."

"Do you think that makes ye unappealing?"

"Aye."

"Then you're mistaken." He rose. "You're a treasure."

"Because of my face." She sounded bitter. He'd already gathered that she loathed her beauty almost as much as she loathed her limp.

"Aye, you're beautiful. But you're more than just a bonny lassie. E.C. Cameron merits respect."

"Perhaps," she said, clearly unconvinced. She went on before he could argue. "There was a young man who developed a *tendre* for me. It was all very innocent. When he saw me, he'd get into such a blushing mess that I dinnae think he said more than two words to me. He used to bring me flowers. But the guard who shared his duties must have told Papa, and my admirer stopped coming to the island. After that, the guards were all older men."

"Nae stolen kisses in the heather?"

It was a risk to mention kisses. He didn't want to frighten her. They were here alone, and if he had even one ounce less honor, she'd be in danger.

Ellen raised her chin in defiance. Will was delighted to see that she didn't look afraid. Perhaps she'd started to trust him a little. "We shouldnae talk about kisses."

"As ye wish," he said, without looking away. Because even if they didn't talk about kisses, he thought about them. He had a sneaking suspicion that she thought about them, too.

He knew what it meant when a lass sent a lad those fluttery sideways looks and when excitement vibrated in her voice. Ellen was aware of him as a male, although whether she meant to act on her attraction was altogether another question.

Could he persuade Ellen to run away with him? He couldn't force her to choose freedom, but the lass who had the courage to establish a purpose to her life on Bortha should be brave enough to snap her chains.

Another silence fell, this one resonant with unspoken desire. As he stared into her eyes, the blue darkened and her breath accelerated until her lovely bosom swelled beneath its pretty floral bodice. A white lace scarf crossed over the front to preserve her modesty, but did nothing to hide her delectable curves.

Ellen inhaled with an audible gasp and turned away to stare at the table. "Would ye like more wine?"

"No, thank you." He remained stock still, afraid that if he dared to approach, she'd take to her heels.

"In that case, I'll...I'll clear up after supper."

Devil take it, she planned to take to her heels anyway. What a swine he was, for scaring her.

"Must ye bring a delightful evening to an end? I promise I'll behave." He backed away to sit on the window seat. At his tacit retreat, the line of her shoulders eased.

She twined her hands together at her waist. "Will ye...will ye tell me more about Achnasheen?"

Will stretched his legs out and adopted a casual air which in no way reflected his interior turmoil. "If ye like."

"It sounds like a lovely place."

"Aye, the most beautiful I know. I say that with authority. I made the grand tour to Italy and France when I was twenty-one."

"Italy?" Curiosity brightened her eyes. "Oh, how lucky ye are."

"Aye." And more aware of his good fortune than ever before, now he'd met Bortha's gorgeous captive.

"Will ye tell me about Florence?" She ventured back to settle beside him. "And Venice. And Rome."

He laughed. "Perhaps no' all of them tonight. I may need to entertain ye for a month, after all."

To his relief, she laughed, too. "I'm sorry. I'm just so eager to hear."

All amusement abandoned him. "Dinnae apologize. You've had so much stolen from ye. If my travelers' tales provide a moment's pleasure, I'm happy to oblige."

Ellen's shining gaze had him struggling to ignore all thought of kisses. Instead, he did his best to summon up his memories.

The candles burned down, and the delicate clock on the mantel chimed two. Will paused in his recounting of a clash with bandits in the Apennines. "Ye must be cursing me to Hades. It's no' far off sunrise."

Ellen had her back against the wall at the end of the seat, and she'd curled her feet under her. Another bottle of wine sat half-full on the table. He'd gone downstairs a couple of hours ago to fetch some claret.

"That was lovely. Ye made me feel like I was with you every step of the way." Her smile was tired, but happy. "You should take up writing."

He shrugged, pleased to give her an interval of ease. Nor had the conversation been all one way. It turned out that the packed bookcases included folios of engravings depicting many of the places he'd visited. "I could never compete with your talent."

"Thank ye." With a shyness that he found enchanting, she lowered her eyes. But then, he found everything about her enchanting. Powerful magic had him in its grip.

"You ken I admire your work. I hope you're going to show me more."

"After I thank you for bringing the world to my doorstep."

"It was my pleasure," he said, surprised how sincerely he meant it.

He'd been disappointed when she'd skittered away from his attempts at flirtation. But he couldn't regret seeing the way that she'd blossomed during the conversation. To think, an evening of mere talk with Ellen Cameron was more enjoyable than tumbling Italy's most famous courtesan.

Will waited for Ellen to stand up and leave, although he'd give anything to extend the evening. Despite the late hour, he wasn't tired at all. Stimulating talk kept him alert. Stimulating talk, and the endless, lazy swirl of desire in his blood.

Right now, his craving was more pleasure than pain. He'd accepted that Ellen had no intention of satisfying him tonight. Even knowing he was a thousand miles from possessing her, he found a piquant enjoyment in his hunger. Two days ago, he'd had no idea she existed. At this moment, he couldn't imagine spending an hour away from her. That was the miracle of attraction.

She didn't make any move to leave. Instead, she stared into the stygian blackness outside. Rain spattered the window, and the wind shrieked. If Will had a choice, he'd make it shriek until Christmas.

Staring at her, he stored up the details of her beauty. No wonder she'd sparked a legend. Her loveliness was breathtaking, especially now when her characteristic wariness faded and her expression turned soft and wistful. He guessed that she was picturing all the places he'd described. Feeling the warm Italian sun on her milky skin. Tasting ripe peaches from the trees of Umbria. Floating down the Grand Canal at sunset in a Venetian gondola.

He already knew that she had a powerful imagination. It had transformed her old nurse's bedtime stories into vivid fiction.

Right now, Will was content to be on Bortha. Nothing in Tuscany compared with Ellen's delicate face, the glow of her eyes, the sheen of candlelight across her tumble of golden curls.

She knew he watched her. Although she avoided his eyes, rose lined her slanted cheekbones. Then he realized that she watched him, too. The darkness outside meant that the window reflected a perfect copy of the two of them on the window seat.

Well, that was interesting. It seemed that he fascinated her, too, perhaps as much as she fascinated him.

But he respected her reserve. For pity's sake, yesterday she'd been ready to shoot him. He'd come a long way since then. If he was any judge of weather – and women – he'd make further progress tomorrow. During what remained of the night, the storm wouldn't abate.

"There havenae been any kisses." Her voice was so low that he had to lean forward to hear her.

The unexpected mention of kisses set his blood thundering. "With your lovelorn guard?"

She turned away from the window and brooded down to where her hands performed a fluttery dance in her lap. "No' with...anyone."

Shock crashed through Will. Although he should have realized. "You've never been kissed."

"No."

She was well into her twenties, old enough to wonder about a man's touch. "Are ye no' curious what it would feel like?"

A soft huff of self-derision. "Of course."

Of course. Curiosity was her essence. He just had to glance at these packed shelves of books to know that.

Was this an invitation? His heart raced, and he had to swallow to loosen a throat dry with excitement. He kept his tone soft and even. "I could kiss ye."

CHAPTER SIX

Will Mackinnon was offering to kiss her.

Every drop of moisture evaporated from Ellen's mouth. She was excited, but she was also afraid. Because while she might be innocent, she was no fool. Will had excellent manners and a way about him that was far too winning, but he was still a man. Her experience of her father told her that men followed their inclinations, with no care for who they damaged in the process.

Will might read any kisses as encouragement to take more. To take everything.

She liked him more than anyone she'd ever met, and that chiseled face with its devil-may-care smile was etched in her soul. He was so beautiful, in a potent, masculine way that turned her knees weak. And he was strong, too, which made his gentleness even sweeter. None of which meant that she'd let him seduce her.

But what about a kiss or two?

If she spent the rest of her life on this godforsaken island, it was likely that she'd never meet anyone else who she wanted to kiss. She was desperate for something to dream about when Will left her, as he must. He might talk about taking her away, but that was just a fantasy. She was trapped here until her father released her. And after ten years, she knew that was never going to happen.

Ellen made a helpless gesture. "If ye do this..."

An understanding smile curved his lips. Those glittering hazel eyes saw far too much. Including how she thrilled at the thought of his lips on hers. "It's just a kiss. I know that."

"I dinnae want..."

"You dinnae want me to mistake what you're inviting."

"Aye."

"Ye have my word that when you ask me to stop, I will."

That wasn't as reassuring as it might be. She'd never kissed a man, but long-buried female instincts insisted that she'd like Will's kisses. It might be harder to ask him to stop than just summoning up the words.

"Have ye kissed a lot of lassies, Mr. Mackinnon?"

He responded with a grunt of laughter. "My fair share. You're no' in the hands of a novice. I'll do my best to give satisfaction, Miss Cameron."

He mocked her. Given that she sounded as if she negotiated the price of a loaf of bread, she couldn't blame him.

"I'm no' worried about that. I'm worried whether I'll measure up."

"I'll make allowances for your inexperience." His lips twitched. "I'm sure a girl who can carry on scholarly discussions with great men across Europe can master the basics. Most people pick up the knack without too much trouble."

"I appreciate your patience," she said with a touch of irony. His teasing made her feel less on edge. "What do I need to do?"

"First ye need to stop calling me Mr. Mackinnon."

Silly to blush at that, especially as she was sure that there would be many much more blush-worthy moments to come. "I suppose ye want to call me Ellen."

"If it's permitted."

And silly to demur over him using her Christian name when he was going to put his hands on her. Nonetheless, granting him the privilege felt like removing a layer of protection that she mightn't be able to get back.

"It's permitted."

"Excellent." He stood and stretched his hands out. "Come here."

Nerves clenched her stomach tight as she stared up at him, hoping to heaven that she was right to trust him. "Can I change my mind?"

"Anytime." His gaze remained steady. "But that would be a pity when you're so curious, and ye have me here to answer your questions."

Her lips quirked in self-deprecation. "I'm being a nitwit, aren't I?"

This time, his smile conveyed a disturbing tenderness that sliced a jagged rift in her heart. There had been so little kindness in her life. "A few collywobbles are to be expected."

"These collywobbles feel like elephants rolling over."

"My advice is throw yourself into the breach."

Her lips trembled as she smiled back. "Of course it is."

"You're no' the only person eager to find out how it would be between us."

"Oh," she squeaked, although she shouldn't be surprised. Hadn't he declared an interest in her from the beginning? What was different with Will Mackinnon was that for the first time, she was interested in return.

With jerky movements, she uncurled her legs from the seat and rose to take his hands. Heat radiated up her arms from his firm grip. She gave a sharp gasp, and her gaze flew up to meet his. Hazel eyes seared into her, and for a long moment, she couldn't breathe as her heart crashed against her ribs over and over.

Ellen wasn't a small woman, but Will towered over her. She hadn't been this close to him before. When she finally managed to gulp in enough air to feed her starving lungs, she caught his scent. Rich and salty, and clean like the ocean.

The ocean kept her prisoner, so she shouldn't find that scent so evocative, but a shudder of pleasure rippled through her. "What should I do now?"

"Follow my lead," he murmured, stepping nearer. He released one of her hands and cradled her face, tilting it toward him.

His touch held the same tenderness that she'd seen in his smile. Disquiet stirred in her stomach, just because this reaction was so devastating. Heaven help her, Will hadn't even kissed her, yet she was close to melting into a puddle of warm honey at his feet.

His hand was gentle on her cheek and before she could question the wisdom of her action, she nestled her face into his palm. His expression changed, became more intent, and a great wave of trepidation swept through her. But before she could force her wobbly legs to move, he bent his auburn head and brushed his lips across hers.

The contact was soft as a feather, as mighty as the blow of a hammer. Her heart turned over in her breast, and every cell in her body tingled. A needy whimper escaped, as he shifted away.

He lifted his other hand to her face, holding her still. But all thought of retreating had fled with that glancing kiss, over far too soon.

"More?" he whispered, the words a puff of warmth across lips that felt preternaturally sensitive. She caught the fresh taste of his breath.

"Aye, please," she whispered back.

She closed her eyes, all the better to dive into the turbulent sea of unparalleled sensation. He lingered, applied a fraction more pressure. Her lips moved against his and clung for a charged instant. This time when he withdrew, her whimper held a note of complaint.

Ellen opened her eyes to meet a gaze the deep green of the rock pools under Bortha's cliffs at low tide. His eyelids were heavy, and his lips were softer and fuller. The changes lent him a dissipated air, and her shiver contained elements of fear and a far more insistent arousal.

He began to kiss each feature, as if he learned through touch what so far he'd only known by sight. His lips traced her cheekbones and the bridge of her nose and the arch of her eyebrows. Everywhere he touched, he lit small fires.

Ellen made an impatient sound deep in her throat and stepped closer, sliding her hands up his arms to broad, sinewy shoulders. When at last he returned his attention to her lips, she sighed and leaned into him. On a soft growl of encouragement, he explored her lips with a thoroughness that set her blood rushing. Only when she copied him did she recall him asking her to follow his lead.

So when the tip of his tongue traced the closed seam, she started but didn't withdraw. When he did it again, she obeyed the silent command and parted to let him in.

He slipped his tongue into her mouth in a flickering foray that wrenched her out of the pervasive fog of pleasure. "Oh..."

He lifted his head. "You dinnae like it?"

"It's...strange."

"I want to taste ye."

Heat surged into her face, and her fingers dug into his shoulders. "That sounds even stranger."

"Are ye feeling daring?"

"Aye." Ocean scent flavored her deep breath. "Aye, I am."

Satisfaction lit his gaze, as if a sunbeam struck one of those mysterious sea pools. Another surge of arousal washed over her. The swift carnality of what they did caught her unprepared.

"Open your mouth for me."

He released her face and twined his arms around her. Without thinking, Ellen fitted herself to his embrace. His touch had an extraordinary effect, as if her bones dissolved and she became all soft surrender.

Will's lips met hers with a heated purpose that made her stomach clench with longing. When his tongue darted into her mouth, the sensation made her shake. This hot intimacy was unlike anything that she'd ever imagined. Her knees turned to water, and she was grateful that he held her so tight. Otherwise she feared she must crumple up in sheer delight.

Tentatively she rubbed her tongue against his. His rumbling approval was the sweetest music she'd ever heard. More confident now, she joined him in the sensual dance of the kiss until she pulled away, dazed and breathless. "Will, that's..."

He was breathless, too, and the smile he gave her felt like more sunlight. "You're sweeter than honeycomb."

She'd given him pleasure. The thought made her happy.

Ellen dared to rise up on her toes, seeking more of those miraculous kisses. The world flared into bright flame, as she lost herself in the incandescent pleasure of a man's mouth on hers. Not just any man. Will Mackinnon who had banished her loneliness with his smile.

When he drew away at last, her heart was galloping fit to burst free of her ribs and a throbbing and unfamiliar weight had set up in the secret parts of her body. She slumped against him, her hands laced behind the strong column of his neck.

"We should stop," he said in a guttural voice that roughened his smooth baritone to gravel.

In his arms, Ellen felt whole and perfect as she never had before. But his words awoke her old uncertainties.

She slid free of his hold and struggled to find her balance. After that astounding pleasure, she was woozy-headed. When she stumbled, shame flooded her, poisoning her earlier joy. Worse when he caught her arm to save her falling.

"Ellen, what is it?"

Her pride had helped her survive her childhood as her father's broken daughter and then ten years of cruel exile. She grabbed for her pride to protect her, as it had protected her before, but those desperate kisses had placed pride out of reach.

Before she could stop herself, she responded honestly. "Is it because I'm a cripple?"

He looked puzzled. "What the hell are ye talking about?"

She should break away. After all, she could stand on her own two feet, however faulty those feet might be. Hadn't she spent her life proving that?

But the touch of Will's hand offered her the only warmth in the whole world, despite the fire blazing in the hearth. She couldn't muster the strength to reject his support.

"You dinnae want to kiss me anymore because I'm...defective." It hurt to say the words, so they emerged like an accusation.

"Good God, what the devil are ye thinking?" He sounded appalled. A muscle jerked in his lean cheek. "And you're no' defective. Ye might walk with a limp, but that doesn't destroy your value as a person."

She wrapped her arms around herself to control the shaking. "Aye, it does," she mumbled, avoiding his eyes.

"I'd dearly love to knock your father to the ground and kick him in the teeth while he's there," Will said in a grim voice that she hadn't heard before.

That wrenched her attention back to his face. He looked furious. "Ye would?"

"Aye. Horsewhipping is too good for the swine. You're an exceptional woman. He should be proud to call ye his daughter. This rejection is his loss, not yours."

"But I'm lame."

"For pity's sake, that doesn't make ye a lesser being. You're beautiful and clever and brave. What does it matter if you cannae dance?"

"Or run or jump or skip."

Compassion tempered the rage in his eyes and for once in her life, pity didn't make her flinch. "I'm sure you miss doing those things, but I think you're marvelous, just as ye are."

She studied him and couldn't mistake his sincerity.

All her life, she'd battled against her father's assessment of her as fundamentally flawed. Did Will offer a different view of her infirmity? As part of a complete picture that wasn't quite so bleak? "You're being kind."

To her surprise, humor set attractive creases around his eyes and curved the mouth that had just taken her to heaven. "Hell, no. I'm never kind."

Surprised, she found herself smiling back. "No, you're a villain of the worst sort. I've always thought so." She made a forlorn gesture, even as she teased him. "So why did ye stop kissing me?"

As he shook his head, his laugh was rueful. "I forget how innocent ye are."

She frowned. "You ken I've never kissed anyone else."

"That's damned exciting." He paused. "You're damned exciting."

She didn't understand what he was trying to tell her, but at least now she accepted that he hadn't stopped because she was lame. "Ye can kiss me again," she said in a faltering voice.

"That's no' a good idea." When he speared one hand through his thick red hair, her fingers itched to smooth it. "And, no, that's no' because I don't want to, but because I want ye too much."

Shock thundered through her. "You're saying you're...aroused?"

His laugh held a beguiling note of self-mockery. "Like the very devil."

"Oh."

"Oh, indeed."

"We're here alone..."

He groaned and closed his eyes. She couldn't doubt that this worldly man was in torment. Over her. Over unloved, awkward, faulty Ellen Cameron.

How delicious.

"Dinnae remind me. I gave ye my word I'd act the gentleman."

"You didnae kiss me like a gentleman."

He'd kissed her as if he wanted to devour her. It had been the most thrilling experience of her life.

Will's eyes opened to reveal a blazing stare. His touch had made her burn. It turned out that those brilliant green-gold eyes could achieve the same effect. "You're so enchanting in my arms that you grind good intentions to dust. I stopped because I couldnae trust myself to respect the limits you placed on me."

Good heavens above, she should be terrified. After all, nobody could save her if he chose to follow his inclinations. But she wasn't terrified. Instead her lonely heart yearned toward him. Because although he'd come close to losing control, he'd stopped. For her sake.

Will Mackinnon turned out to be that rarest of beasts, an honorable man. Which presented a problem Ellen had never imagined she'd face.

"Are ye saying you willnae kiss me again?" The prospect of living without his kisses struck her as tragic.

He slumped onto the window seat. "That would be wise."

"Because I tempt ye." Despite his barely hidden despair at their dilemma, the idea seemed preposterous.

"Aye. Too much."

Her elation fading, she sank down beside him. Now that he'd kissed her, she wanted him to kiss her again. And again. But she knew what happened between men and women. She knew that hungry kisses were the overture to sexual congress.

He hadn't kissed her like a gentleman. He'd kissed her like a man who intended to take her to bed and join his body with hers.

"I cannae risk a child," she said in a deliberate tone. "My father would kill me if he ever discovered that I was here alone with ye. He already counts me as a disgrace to the Camerons."

Will studied her, his gaze reaching right to her soul. "Are ye saying you'd like to go further?"

Wanton blood rushed into her cheeks, but she managed to keep her voice steady. "I'm saying I liked kissing ye and perhaps I'd like to discover what other pleasures we can enjoy together. I'm also saying it's impossible. Even if my father didnae kill me, what life could a child have here? It would be too cruel to subject another living being to this captivity. Or my father would remove any child from my care and foster it somewhere that the shame doesn't attach to the Laird of Inchgallen."

"That would break your heart."

"Aye, it would. No' to mention I wouldn't consign my worst enemy to my father's care, let alone a child of my body."

Will continued to study her with that unwavering attention that felt like a caress. "Ye know," he said slowly, "there are things we can do together that won't result in a baby, and that will leave you as virginal as ye are now."

CHAPTER SEVEN

Will knew that what he said only set him up for more torture. Even if it was a torture interlaced with sizzling pleasure.

Kissing Ellen had been a revelation. She was passionate and gloriously responsive. The prospect of seeing her achieve her first climax under his hand was worth any torment.

Because he was already in torment. He wanted to claim Ellen Cameron as his in the most essential way. He wanted to thrust deep into her slender body and fill her with his seed. When she spoke of making a child together, he longed to see her grow large and round and contented, while his baby nestled safe in her womb.

Beside him, she frowned as she considered what he suggested. More torture. She was both too far away for his liking and too close for comfort. "But will that no' be difficult for you?"

He bit back a sardonic laugh. Difficult? It was going to be hell. But hell with a fair dollop of heaven mixed in, too. "There are things I can do to find relief."

"But will it be enough?"

He shrugged. "It has to be. I'd dearly love to touch ye and show you some of the pleasures you've been missing."

Her troubled expression didn't ease. "And ye won't..."

Dear God, he hoped that overmastering desire wasn't about to make a liar of him. "Ye have my word."

"I'd have to trust ye."

"Aye." The clock on the mantel struck three. "Think about it and tell me in the morning."

Her lips twitched. "It is the morning."

"Well, after the sun comes up." Not that he'd caught a glimpse of the sun since he'd arrived. Which suited him fine. Right now, the sun was his enemy. The sun meant a return of her guardians and an end to his time with her.

She directed a long, serious look at him. "I dinnae want to leave you."

Gratification flooded him. If Ellen could bring herself to make such an admission, she was close to saying yes. "Then I'll stay."

"I'm no' ready to invite you into my bed."

"We could lie down here." He gestured to the window seat. "I'd like to hold ye in my arms."

"Just...hold?"

"Aye."

"Ye must think that I'm a ninny to hesitate."

He thought that she'd known too many useless men, starting with her dear papa, but that was a discussion for another time. "I think that if you stay with me, ye grant me a great privilege."

"You're far too charming." Ellen sent him a disapproving look. "I never trust ye when you say such things. Sweet words like that must have led many a maiden astray at Achnasheen."

He smiled, appreciating the challenge. "Are they likely to lead a maiden astray on Bortha?"

"No, she's much more stalwart."

Delight filled him. She was indeed.

Wasn't he the world's luckiest laddie to have her to himself? But only while the wind blew. He had such little time to gain her trust, then persuade her to leave. She was a long way from sailing away in his company. Perhaps if he could turn sensual pleasure into an addiction, he might lure her to escape.

He'd do his damnedest.

Will stretched one arm out. "Come and rest in my embrace, my bonny. I'll keep ye warm and safe. Any other decisions can wait."

Her expression turned uncertain, and he waited for her to tell him that she'd changed her mind. He didn't underestimate what he demanded. She'd known him little more than a day, and she wasn't someone who lowered her barriers just for the asking.

A wide yawn resulted in a very un-Ellen-like giggle. "That says it all, I think."

She slid across the seat and snuggled against him. As his arm encircled her, his heart gave a mighty thud of satisfaction. Her scent surrounded him. Lavender soap. A hint of old books. Something fresh and warm that was Ellen's alone.

He raised her chin. "Good night, Ellen."

Her beautiful ice-blue eyes were heavy with weariness, but she managed a smile. "Good night, Will."

He dipped his head to kiss her. Their lips clung for a sweet instant before she withdrew. She laid her head on his chest, over the place where his heart beat with yearning for her.

Will stirred to the gray light that had become familiar since he'd come to this isolated tower. He extended full-length against the window, and a soft bundle of femininity pressed tight against him. His nose was buried in a silky mass of blond hair.

Sometime during the night, they must have shifted to lie down, although he couldn't remember moving. The narrow seat provided a surprisingly comfortable bed, when he had Ellen's back to his chest and her head resting on his arm.

The fire had burned down to embers and the room was cold, but he wasn't yet ready to relinquish his precious armful. Outside, the wind wailed. He said a silent prayer for the gale to keep up, although given his immoral intentions, perhaps it might be best to keep the Almighty away from his plans.

With a drowsy grumble, Ellen stirred. When his embrace firmed, she shifted again but didn't move away, praise heaven. "You're awake," she said softly.

"Aye."

"Ye kept your word." Her rump bumped against his swollen prick, and he bit back a groan.

He set his jaw against his body's demands. "Ye can trust me."

"Mmm," she said, and he hid a wince at the noncommittal tone.

Will dropped into another doze. The next time he opened his eyes, he guessed it must be somewhere around nine. He couldn't see the clock from where he lay. Prosaic needs prodded him, but he did his best to ignore them.

Ellen couldn't know quite how much it cost him to stick to his principles right now. But in his short time on the island, he'd reached a number of conclusions, not least that Ellen had been bullied far too often. She deserved the chance to make her own choices. He just hoped to God that she chose to give him his way.

This time when she moved, it was with more purpose. With reluctance, he slid his arms away from her. "Ye mean to get up."

"Aye. Aye, I do."

She pushed free and rose to her feet. He regarded her with bleary pleasure. She was delightfully rumpled. The stylish gown was wrinkled, and her hair was half out of its knot. She looked younger and more approachable, a different creature altogether from the virago who had threatened to shoot him when he climbed through her window.

Color flushed her cheekbones, and she raised a shaking hand to her tumble of hair. "I must look a complete disaster."

This unexpected vanity sparked tenderness in Will's heart, and he found himself smiling at her like a lunatic. "You're lovely. You're always lovely."

She waved away his compliment. "And you're always gallant."

He sat up and placed one hand over his flip-flopping heart. "On my honor, gallantry is too much to ask of a man who's just woken up after only a few hours' sleep. I speak the truth."

Seeing her so ruffled and untidy, he couldn't help thinking of bed sport. His hands itched to unpin her hair and unlace the elaborate gown to reveal the curves beneath.

"Flatterer." Her husky laugh made his balls heavier. She pushed her hair back from her face, and the eyes she leveled on him were dark with weariness. Weariness and a sensual awareness that crashed through him like an avalanche. "Whereas ye look as godlike as ever. It's no' fair when I'm sure I look like a scarecrow planted out in a hurricane."

It was his turn to blush, something he couldn't remember doing since he was an awkward boy with a penchant for his Drummond cousin Martha. Beneath his abashment, he was mighty pleased that Ellen liked the way he looked. It was the first time that she'd admitted any such weakness. "Och, go on with ye, you daft lassie."

Her smile conveyed a tinge of smugness. "I'm going upstairs to wash and change. I'll see ye in the kitchen for breakfast."

He cast a derisive glance at his shirt. "I think a man who is truly godlike would have a clean shirt."

"I'll wash it, if ye like. It should dry in front of the fire."

"Thank you."

"I'll see ye later."

She didn't move straightaway, just stood there while her eyes ate him up. Will curled his hands over the edge of the window seat to stop himself from jumping up and grabbing her and kissing her into a fluster.

Ellen was yet to mention last night's kisses or his offer to go further than kisses. Something stopped him from asking for an answer. Perhaps a shameful fear of the blow that she'd strike if she said no.

The strange stasis continued, until she released her breath in a hiss. She turned toward the staircase leading up to the bedroom he was yet to see. Will realized that he, too, had been holding his breath. His head swam as he sucked air into his empty lungs. He'd never met a woman who stopped the breath in his chest. Ellen did it without even trying.

When Will arrived with his shirts in his hand, Ellen was standing at the hearth, stirring the porridge and looking enchantingly domestic. At his entrance, she turned and her eyes went as round as saucers.

Her gaze focused on his bare chest. "Oh, my..."

To his chagrin, he found himself blushing again. This lassie had him in such a dither. When she licked her lips with innocent voluptuousness, he got even more steamed up, despite spending the last half hour lecturing himself on the necessity for control.

"You're burning the porridge," he said, finding it difficult to speak through the tumult in his blood.

She still stared at him as if he was an apparition. "What?"

"The porridge?"

"The porridge?" She blinked and went as red as a rowanberry. Heaven help them, they were as bad as each other. "Oh, the porridge."

She turned so fast that she wobbled. Before he could remind himself that she didn't like anyone making allowances for her lameness, he lunged forward to catch her elbow.

For a charged moment, she remained trembling in his grasp. The immediate heat between them was as shocking as lightning in a clear sky. He stepped closer to kiss her, even though he'd resolved to avoid physical persuasion.

She leaned toward him, then caught her breath and straightened. "The porridge."

"Aye," he said, releasing her. His heart raced like a riptide. He guessed hers might, too.

Will had never felt so shaken in his life. He'd known the first time he saw her that she was a prize worth winning, but this pursuit of Fair Ellen of the

Isles was becoming the most important thing he'd ever done.

With a concentration they didn't deserve, she stirred the oats. Whatever had happened just now had disturbed her as profoundly as it disturbed him.

"Put...put your shirts over a chair."

"Thank ye for washing them for me." Did she notice how unnatural he sounded?

"It's nae trouble." Her voice was higher than usual. "Sit down, and I'll get your breakfast."

Honey and cream turned the humble meal into a feast, but conversation remained stilted. Which reminded Will of how easily they'd filled the hours yesterday.

His craving for Ellen meant that conversation, no matter how fine, could no longer satisfy him. Had it been a mistake to kiss her? He knew now how she tasted and how her passion flared into wildfire. He knew the sound of her soft murmurs of pleasure.

It had been difficult enough keeping his hands off Ellen before. Now it was nigh impossible.

She was shy with him in a way she hadn't been yesterday. When she spoke, she jumped from topic to topic, and she avoided his eyes. This morning, she'd chosen a plainer dress, too. Yesterday's ensemble could have graced a smart London street. Today she wore a pale green gown with a demure collar. Her hair was confined in a severe knot.

Will wondered what signals she meant to send. Was she hinting that her answer must be no? Or was she trying to play down her extraordinary beauty? If so, it was a miserable failure. Even in sackcloth and ashes, her golden perfection would shine through.

He and Ellen balanced on a dizzying precipice. The question was would she take his hand and dare the terrifying drop, or would she retreat to safety?

Last night, he'd hoped he had a chance of gaining her consent. This morning, he wasn't so optimistic.

She rose to collect their empty bowls. "I must go and milk Buttercup."

He glanced up, although again she avoided his eyes. "Let me do it."

"You're a guest."

A wry smile twisted his lips. "No' exactly. More an intruder."

Her faint smile filled him with relief. "No, ye stopped being an intruder yesterday."

By God, that sounded like a concession. He started to rise from his chair, then subsided when he reminded himself that he'd sworn not to put any pressure on her. "So let me look after Buttercup."

"Thank you."

Will stood and left. It was either that or seize the girl in his arms and kiss her senseless.

Buttercup was bellowing in complaint when Will braved the weather to reach the byre. The storm showed no sign of abating. He couldn't help taking nefarious pleasure in that fact.

It might be torture to keep his hands off Ellen. It would be worse to leave her.

"I'm sorry, old girl." He set up the bucket and settled on the stool. The familiar scents of hay and cattle surrounded him as he milked the cow. "I ken I'm late."

At least the air was warmer in here. "It's been a very strange wee while."

He started to tell the cow about everything that had happened, although he spared Buttercup the details of those damned fine kisses.

"The question is what do I do now," he said in a musing voice. Buttercup had proven a good listener as he'd milked her and organized fodder and water. "Do I pounce? Or do I hold back and let Ellen decide what we do next? The lassie liked my kisses, so pouncing might convince her to yield. She was nervous this morning, so I fear if I leave the decision up to the lady, her fears will win out, which would be an infernal shame. Especially as she's so innocent, she doesnae ken what she's denying herself. On the other hand, I like to think I'm a man of honor and pouncing might frighten her. I'd cut my throat before I do that."

Will paused as if Buttercup replied. He began to muck out the stall. With luck, hard work might take the edge off his frustration.

He stopped to catch his breath. "Buttercup, what do ye think?"

But while Buttercup was an excellent listener, she wasn't half so handy as a conversationalist. Her silence was no help at all.

He sighed and leaned one forearm on the shovel's wooden handle, as he regarded the cow with weary interest. "Is it pounce or politeness, my friend? Which is the most likely to gain the favor of Fair Ellen of the Isles?"

The voice that replied was wry and feminine – and didn't come from Buttercup. "My vote is for pounce."

CHAPTER EIGHT

Ellen smothered a laugh as Will whirled to face her, his expression a picture of dismay. "How long have ye been there?"

"Long enough." It had been enlightening and surprisingly flattering to hear him describe her in such florid terms. She'd wondered if perhaps she plunged fathoms deep into attraction because she was too inexperienced to protect herself. It was a relief to hear that this conflagration of desire left the much more worldly Will Mackinnon just as bewildered. A relief and a worry. Because she feared that there might be only one end to their time together, and she wasn't convinced she was ready to be ruined.

"I was hoping Buttercup might have some advice." He was charming all the time. It turned out that he was particularly charming when he was embarrassed. Will was in general a confident man, but the hint of bashfulness was far too disarming to a lady struggling to keep her head.

"I wouldnae trust to Buttercup who's a giddy, reckless beast, no' to be relied upon at all. She's notorious as the wild lassie of Bortha." Although

Ellen had a strong premonition that there was only one wild lassie on Bortha, and it wasn't Buttercup.

A sardonic auburn eyebrow arched in enquiry. "Is that so?"

"Aye." She glanced around the stable, taking in the evidence of Will's industry.

She'd already noticed how magnificent he looked with his broad back bare to her gaze and that flamboyant hair cascading over his shoulders. Now that he turned in her direction, she had to fight not to stare at the brawny expanse of chest with its light covering of curly red hair.

She was almost sorry she'd washed his shirts. Giving him a shirt seemed like a sin against nature, when he looked so superb without one.

His disconcerted air faded, and her nerves revived as his eyes sharpened on her. "Did ye mean it?"

Heaven help her, she'd become so dreamy, drooling over the picture he made, that she'd lost the thread of the conversation. "Mean what?"

"The pouncing bit."

She blushed and told herself to demur, but what emerged was a single word. "Aye."

Ellen braced for Will to grab her with those hard, capable hands, but he studied her as if he set out to translate her from the Latin. "Ye were really jumpy this morning."

"This is such new territory for me." Her gesture conveyed her turmoil. "Yesterday I'd never been kissed. Today I'm considering letting ye take liberties with my body."

His confidence definitely returned. A hint of triumph tilted that expressive mouth. "Only considering?"

"Curse ye, Will. No, I've gone beyond considering. I've made up my mind."

His shout of laughter made her scowl at him, although the woeful reality was that she couldn't resist him. "I'm delighted to hear it." He glanced around the dim space. "I've finished here. If ye give me a chance to wash off the stench of the farmyard, I'm at your disposal."

Ellen wasn't sure that she wanted him washing. She stood close enough to pick up the scent of clean male sweat, and the dirt on his skin stirred her primitive instincts. An intriguing shadow of a beard emphasized his sculpted jaw. This was a man who could ravish her into oblivion.

She reminded herself that she intended to stop well short of ravishment, but she couldn't contain a disappointed note. "I have a fancy for the rugged stablehand."

This time, his laugh held a note of shock, but desire flared in his eyes as he flung the shovel away and stepped closer. "No' our first time. Let me carry back the milk and make myself fit for ye."

First time? A universe of possibilities opened up before her. Exciting possibilities. Alarming possibilities.

She backed away, then cursed her skittishness. "Perhaps we should wait until later this afternoon. Otherwise we'll have to stop what we're doing and come out to milk Buttercup again."

"Already asking for a reprieve?"

"Maybe."

His eyes were kind, as they so often were. "Pounce, but no' yet?"

"Do ye mind?"

He shook his head. "No. I'll survive another couple of hours. I hope."

Ellen gulped in a breath tinged with the scent of a healthy, active man and swayed toward him, wondering whether she was mad to put off the moment. "Do I...do I need to do anything?"

"Just come to me with a generous heart and a promise that if it all becomes too frightening, you'll tell me."

Her eyes widened. "Frightening?"

"I intend more than kisses."

Ellen knew that he did. She linked her hands at her waist to hide their trembling. "Ye want to join me in my bedroom."

"If you'll permit. The window seat isn't adequate to my intentions."

Goodness gracious. Her imagination wasn't adequate to what was coming. "Should I undress?"

"Whatever makes ye most comfortable."

Her laugh was strangled. "I cannae think I'm going to be comfortable, whatever I do."

His expression turned somber. "You dinnae have to do this, Ellen."

She swallowed to ease a throat that was so tight, it ached. "Aye, I do," she said in a raw voice.

When the color of his eyes deepened to gold, she saw that he recognized the magnitude of her confession. "I'll keep ye safe."

She had a sinking feeling that it was far too late to talk about safety. She'd abandoned safety when she hadn't shot him. She'd certainly abandoned any possibility of safety when she let him kiss her.

"Thank you," she said, still in that reedy tone. Her racing heart made her dizzy, and her shallow breaths left her starved of air.

He leaned forward to kiss her. While it wasn't like yesterday's passion, heat sizzled through her. "Walk with me back to the tower."

"Aye." She reached for his hand, uncaring that he'd been hard at work and it was dirty.

Ellen perched on the edge of the large bed that she'd never shared with another soul. Never had she imagined that she'd share it with a man. Queasy panic churned in her stomach.

A fire burned in the hearth. It might be summer, but this storm carried all of winter's fury. She'd removed her gown and stays and petticoats, but left her shift on. A bronze velvet peignoir lent her an illusion of modesty. It covered her like a frock, except that one tug on the sash would loosen it.

Undressing and washing had taken an age, because of her shaking, fumbling hands. She was more nervous than she'd ever been in her life, even when one of the suitors had tried to break into the tower with his armed band. On that occasion, she'd lit the beacon on the ramparts to summon extra men from Inchgallen.

Even if she wanted rescuing, the beacon wouldn't help her today.

Sightlessly she stared out the large window, bigger than the one downstairs. How many hours had she spent surveying that empty sea, lamenting her loneliness? How lonely would her life be after Will left? He talked about taking her away, but she couldn't see herself surviving anywhere else, except on this isolated island.

Despite her fears, she never thought of changing her mind about letting Will touch her. She now wished that he'd taken her up on her request in the byre, when she told him to pounce. Several hours' delay allowed too much time to think about what she was about to do with a man who remained a stranger.

Except he didn't feel like a stranger. Yesterday had been the most wonderful experience of her life, culminating in those glorious kisses. Then he'd held her close all night. The notion of losing him before she explored this new sensual landscape was unbearable.

It was too late to retreat. Will Mackinnon would lead her into a world of pleasure, and she didn't plan to muster a whisper of denial.

When she heard him on the stairs, she gave a start, although she'd awaited his arrival since she'd left him in the study.

At the top of the staircase, he paused to lean one shoulder against the wall. Bare-chested and in his kilt, he looked like a hero from one of the stories in her book. With faint regret, she noticed that he'd taken the time to shave.

Brilliant eyes swept across her. "Ye look terrified out of your mind."

A choked laugh escaped. "I'm ready to run for the hills." She paused. "Or the hill, given there's only one on Bortha."

"You're in control here."

Her gesture expressed confusion. "It doesnae feel like it."

He didn't venture closer. "Are ye sure you want to do this?"

Right now with an alien masculine presence invading her bedroom, she wasn't sure at all. But the prospect of Will sailing away without satisfying her curiosity was worse than her fear.

She raised her chin. "I want ye to...touch me."

"I want to touch ye, too. More than I've ever wanted to touch another woman."

His confession astounded her. "Really?"

"Really." A rueful smile. "Ye turn my world upside down, Fair Ellen."

Years of accepting that she was a lesser being should refute his statement, but as she stared into his intent gaze, she believed him. Even the Fair Ellen name didn't sting as it almost always did. His lilting baritone rang with sincerity. She'd never understand why, but this spectacular man suffered with his need of her.

She forced herself upright on legs that felt like sodden wool. She wanted this man. Now he'd come to her, she refused to cringe like a coward. "Then ye are welcome, Will Mackinnon."

He must see that she'd committed herself to this path, because his expression eased. "Thank you."

His avid gaze conducted a thorough inspection of her. When she saw the joy that he took in her, her heart swelled with anticipation and gathering certainty. Chance had blown him to her island. Chance, for once, had been a benevolent influence.

He waved a hand in her direction. "I'm so pleased ye didnae let down your hair. The thought of unpinning all that gold silk has fueled my dreams."

Ellen might have decided that she was doing this, but her hand shook when she touched the plain knot. "I didnae ken."

He straightened from his elegant slouch and stepped forward. "You ken now."

Her heart gave a drunken lurch at his intent expression. In this pretty room full of feminine gewgaws, he seemed impossibly tall and strong. She waited for him to seize her, the way he had when he'd kissed her last night. But he remained still and watchful.

"Meet me," he murmured, the soft words as weighty as a punch to the solar plexus.

Half-resentful surprise rushed through her. It seemed that he'd meant it when he said she was in control. He expected her to take responsibility for what they did together today – and until the storm died away. If she hoped to salve her conscience by saying that he'd lured her into yielding, she was to be disappointed.

When she took a step, she couldn't help wincing at her lack of grace. She cast him a pleading glance. "I'm close to the bed."

"We willnae be in the bed for a little while yet." His smile conveyed the tenderness that she'd always recognized as his greatest weapon against her. Her aching heart yearned toward him, starving for the sweetness that flowed alongside his potency.

She sucked in a breath and took another step, surer this time. He wanted her complete self, flaws and qualities alike. As her gaze locked with his, she read acceptance. Acceptance that she'd never found before.

Ellen drew her first full breath in what felt like hours and squared her shoulders. Her next few steps were firm and determined. When she was mere inches away, he reached out and caught her up in a kiss that set the air on fire.

CHAPTER NINE

Will took his time kissing Ellen, delighting in her swift and heated response. She was like flame in his embrace. Only when she was boneless with pleasure, draped across him like a scarf, did he begin to caress her body. He kept kissing her in a playful game that he hoped would stop her thinking too much about where his hands wandered.

Delicately, because he was so desperate not to frighten her, he ran his hands down that long, slender back and shaped the graceful arch of her hips. Then he dared to cup the luscious globes of her buttocks.

She murmured soft encouragement against his lips and pressed closer. Arousal shuddered through him, and his cock swelled in response. But he fought back the tide. Today was all about giving Ellen pleasure, not seeking his own satisfaction.

With a brief brush of his lips across her forehead and nose and chin, he drew back. “Let me take down your hair.”

Her blue eyes were cloudy with desire. After that eon of kissing, her lips were full and soft and damp. A beguiling flush marked her slanted cheekbones.

The world called her fair. Seeing her like this, Will realized that the world had no idea of just how unforgettable the captive maiden of Bortha was.

"Aye," she whispered, although nobody could hear them or witness how they yielded to an attraction that roared out of control.

Will already knew that this girl was special. But even recognizing that, he was surprised at how his hands trembled when he raised them to that rumpled mass of gilt blond hair. He wasn't by any means a rake, but he'd known his share of women, and he accounted himself a skillful, considerate lover. But those earlier, lighthearted encounters belonged to a different universe. Now every second, every word, every action held a significance that shook his world.

When he'd started to touch her, impatience had gripped him. He thirsted to explore her breasts, to see her naked, to discover the secret hollows between her legs. But now time spooled out before him like a long, silken ribbon.

What a gift Ellen bestowed upon him. He owed her pleasure beyond her most extravagant dreams. With a wholehearted unselfishness which to his shame he'd never before devoted to a lover, he placed himself at Ellen's service.

He drew a pin from her hair and watched in wonder as one long tress uncoiled down her neck and across her velvet-covered breast. He dropped the pin to the red and blue Turkey carpet. He'd become accustomed to the luxury hidden inside the tower's unwelcoming exterior. But this bedroom was like a treasure cave, with opulent fabrics and tapestries and decorations. Although nothing could compare with the greatest treasure by far, Ellen herself.

With the same care, he slid another pin free. She stood quiet beneath his hands, although she was trembling. He hoped more with excitement than fear.

Soon a sumptuous cascade of silk cloaked her shoulders. In an ecstasy of delight, he buried his hands in her hair, lifting handfuls and letting them drift down like spun gold. "You're so lovely."

Usually she bridled when he commented on her beauty, but this time she smiled. "I'm glad ye take pleasure in me."

"Och, I do, lassie." He smiled back. "I do."

With languorous sensuality, her slender hands trailed up his bare arms. Wherever her touch landed, it sparked heat. When he kissed her, she responded with an ardor that revealed how titillating she found his slow seduction.

By heaven, it worked on him, too.

Will stepped back far enough to untie the sash on her peignoir. He grunted with self-disgust when he fumbled at the knot. With her warm, floral scent swimming in his head, the simple task turned out not to be so simple after all.

"See the state I'm in? I'm quite mad for ye."

She laid a soft touch on his hand. The tender brush of her fingers jammed the breath in his throat. "I like that you dinnae take this lightly."

"Lightly?" Another huff of wry amusement escaped. "I feel like the world is about to end."

"That sounds dreadful."

His attention lifted from the knot's infernal puzzle. "Trust me, the world ends in a dazzling explosion."

She frowned, not understanding. How would she? "That still doesnae sound good."

"Och, it's very good indeed. You'll see what I mean, if I ever manage to untie this pestilential belt."

Her husky little giggle tightened his balls. "Let me."

To his surprise, the innocent lady released the sash in a second. Her fingers retained the skill that the experienced lover lacked.

Her robe gaped over a transparent shift as fine as a cobweb. His unsteady hands pushed the heavy peignoir off her shoulders. With a whisper, it slid to the floor.

"Ellen..."

Will's breath snagged in his lungs, making speech impossible. He'd never seen anything so lovely as Ellen at that moment. Even lovelier was the shy surrender shining in her blue eyes. From the first, she'd tugged at his emotions. Her beauty was the least of it, alluring as that was. His soul yearned to possess her strength and her passion and her incisive mind.

Now, as she stood quaking with nerves, but proud, too, he recognized that this wasn't just another woman. This was *the* woman. The other half of his soul. The lady he wanted to take back to Achnasheen as his wife, his chatelaine, the mother of his children.

His heart expanded, as the blood of centuries of conquering warriors welled up to claim her. He was going to get her off this island. He was going to marry her. He was going to keep her by his side for the rest of his life – and in heaven, too, if the Good Lord was merciful.

Fair Ellen of the Isles mightn't know it yet, but the day that Will Mackinnon's boat beached on the rocky shores of Bortha, her fate was sealed.

Her hands fluttered in front of her body. "What...what are you thinking?"

Devil take him, he must be glaring at her the way a lion glared at his lunch. No wonder she looked more terrified by the second. But over these last minutes, his world had shifted on its axis. He needed time to catch his breath and find his balance.

Balance? That was a joke. From his first sight of her, Ellen had sent him reeling. He suspected that she'd always keep him on his toes. He, like his parents, was going to have a volatile marriage. He couldn't wait.

Which meant he needed to employ every ounce of sensual guile to convince her to accept his proposal. If he mentioned the word "forever" now, she'd run a mile.

Pleasure would light the way to wooing her. She'd be his before he was done – and not just while the storm raged outside.

"I'm plotting how to proceed," he murmured.

She gave a startled squeak. "That's no' altogether reassuring."

He feared that the smile curving his lips might still be a wee bit too carnivorous. "It's exciting, though."

His boldness made her laugh. She was a brave creature. She'd had to be to survive her exile. "Aye, the way standing on a cliff in the midst of a gale is exciting."

That was his girl. "You're no' made to hide away and live a dull life. You're made for cliffs and gales and the wide, open ocean."

A troubled frown shadowed her features. "You're wrong. I've been hidden away most of my life."

He caught her fidgeting hands. "But does your soul no' long for more? I willnae believe it if you say it doesn't."

"I've been curious, of course. But I've come to accept my lot."

"Liar."

Startled she stepped back, the uneven movement reminding him that he hadn't yet persuaded her that she was fit to take on the world. Fit? This woman was born to reign and astonish. "I've tried to accept it."

"Then stop. You're a fighter. Keep fighting."

Ellen regarded him in puzzlement, although she left her hands in his. "Ye think you know me awfully well for someone who only met me two days ago."

It was a reprimand, one he no doubt deserved. His arrogance might yet lead him astray. Will reminded himself that he couldn't rush his campaign to show her he'd make a great husband.

But dear God, he only had her to himself while the storm raged. He couldn't brook too much delay. "I knew ye the first time I saw you."

It was true. His soul had recognized her as the jewel that he'd sought all his life. His mind had taken a little longer to catch up. That was how it went sometimes.

Her lips firmed and to his horror, she broke away and bent to pick up the crumpled peignoir. "Ye know, I'm starting to wonder if I want to do this. You're a wee bit too cocky about your rights."

Damn it, he'd rushed his fences. Now he looked likely to take a painful spill from his high horse. He caught her arm, keeping his touch gentle because he didn't want to frighten her. Also because along with his male impulse to conquer, he harbored a huge lake of tenderness for her. When his desire had slammed down so hard at the same time as a compulsion to protect her, he should have realized that something unprecedented was happening.

"Don't."

She went still under his hold but didn't release the peignoir. With a haughtiness that made him want to kiss the insolence from her, she arched her eyebrows. He respected her refusal to submit to him without conditions. He respected it, even as he acknowledged that he'd lost a good deal of ground.

Another reminder that he needed to be careful.

"Don't?" she asked in the voice that had threatened to shoot a bullet into him.

Will swallowed and lowered his voice. "Please."

A silence fell. Her eyes searched his face. "Ye have nae rights over me that I don't grant, and I can withdraw those rights in a second if I wish."

"I accept that."

"I might be curious about what we can do together, but yielding to that curiosity doesnae mean you own me."

"I accept that, too. While I hope to open a world of pleasure to ye, I'm at your command." Right now, he wouldn't wager a groat on even kissing her again. And that would be a sodding calamity. "Ye said you trusted me. You've trusted me so far."

"But something has changed." She remained ill at ease. "I feel it."

She was so clever. And so attuned to him, which boded well for their future. He wasn't alone in feeling this powerful affinity.

"You're standing in front of me, close to naked. That's a change, one that receives my hearty approval." He tried a smile, but she'd gone back to being stern.

Her troubled gaze latched onto his face. "Dinnae hurt me, Will."

Any urge to humor fled, and he tightened his grip in protest. “You’ll like what I do, I promise.”

Her lips flattened, as he shifted under her concentrated regard. The uncompromising inspection wasn’t altogether comfortable.

“I dinnae mean physically. I’m sure ye can take me to heaven and back. You’re that sort of man. I might be an innocent, but I’m also a woman, and all my instincts tell me you’re an accomplished lover.”

He frowned. That didn’t sound like praise for his prowess. “I swear that I’ll never speak a word about what passes between us.”

Ellen didn’t look satisfied, but she didn’t push for more. He recognized the risks that she took with him. She was safe, but only his actions and time would prove that.

She raised her chin. “Then give me pleasure as ye promised.”

Instead of leaping to obey, Will studied her with the same attention she’d devoted to him. “If I do anything you dinnae like, I’ll stop.”

He hoped to hell he would. Already her subtle lavender fragrance and the softness of her skin beneath his hand had his blood clamoring.

To his surprise, faint amusement tinged her austere expression. “I have a feeling I’ll like everything ye do.”

“I’ll do my best.”

“Show me.”

CHAPTER TEN

When determination filled Will's striking face, Ellen wanted to back away like a frightened rabbit. She felt torn between her natural urge to stay safe and a devouring curiosity that made her blood rush. She was also painfully conscious that she only wore a transparent shift. Will Mackinnon now knew just what her body looked like.

He said that she held the power, but with every second, she fell further under his spell. He was experienced. She was innocent. He was large and strong. She was small and fragile. He risked nothing in this encounter. She risked everything.

Yet even knowing those things, she couldn't summon up a denial. Curiosity held her here, and something stronger, a physical attraction that had struck the first time she beheld this complicated, red-haired adventurer. An attraction that had only strengthened since.

She wanted Will to touch her. She wanted his kisses. She didn't want to spend their time together hiding how she ached to be in his arms.

The moment for proud pretense had passed.

So when he stepped forward and caught her up against him with a fervor that both terrified and thrilled her, she yielded. When he kissed her with a heady passion that made her shake, she opened her mouth and sucked in his tongue and pressed closer to that impressive chest with its light covering of russet hair.

The evocative ocean scent made her head reel. Under that, something musky, familiar from his kisses last night. Male arousal.

His hands explored her, running down her arms, shaping her waist and hips, kneading her buttocks. Everywhere he touched, he made her burn, until surely she must flare up into a column of flame. As her breasts crushed into his chest, her nipples tightened. She wanted him to touch her there.

More wicked than that, needy heat concentrated in the private place between her legs. Will made her feel restless and empty, as if she'd die unless he filled her.

Ellen struggled to remind herself that he wouldn't be filling her. He'd promised, and while she might be a fool, she believed that he'd keep his word. But as his mouth ravaged hers and his hands discovered her dips and curves, every muscle softened in preparation for possession.

His lips performed an enchanting dance across her face, before they trailed an incendiary line down her neck. She whimpered when he discovered the place where her neck met her shoulder. The scrape of his teeth against that sensitive hollow made her quake.

Her knees turned to soup, and she clung to his sinewy shoulders to stop herself buckling to the floor. With every touch of those hard, competent hands, curiosity stirred more powerfully.

When he'd kissed her, she thought that she learned the meaning of desire. Now she realized how he'd held back. He didn't hold back now. Through his kilt, she felt his insistent hardness. That should frighten her, but she trusted him. More, she loved knowing that she excited him as much as he excited her.

As he raked his hands through her hair and he raised her head for more kisses, she launched her own exploration. Her gaze had eaten him up since she'd first seen him, even when she'd feared him. The impact of those extraordinary looks had only become more powerful. Now touch discovered what sight had hankered after.

She ran her hands down his powerful neck and the muscles of his arms. The delicious warmth of his skin made her palms tingle. Eager fingers threaded his mane of hair. She pulled back from his seeking lips to stroke the expanse of his chest. Discovering firm pectorals and male nipples that hardened under her seeking fingers. His reaction made her nipples tighten to the point of pain.

"You're so beautiful," she thought. When he grunted, she realized she'd spoken aloud.

"Och, can a man be beautiful?"

She dared to lean in and kiss his chest, as her hands drifted down his ridged abdomen to the thick black belt that held up his kilt. Apart from his silky hair, he was hard everywhere, thrillingly so. Yet his touch at her waist was tender. Her heart compressed, as she realized that even now, he leashed his strength to protect her.

"You are." Ellen lifted her head until her gaze met his. His eyes were dark and heavy, and drooping eyelids lent him a sensual air. "The way a storm is beautiful, or a wild ocean, or a shower of shooting stars. Everything untamed and powerful and magnificent."

His expression changed to startled pleasure, before he kissed her with an intensity that had her toes curling. "I'm flattered."

"It's true," she murmured, twining her arms around his neck and stretching up in pursuit of more kisses.

His touch changed, became more commanding. He curved his hands around her buttocks and a draft against the back of her legs told her that he'd raised the hem of her shift. When his hands met her bare rump, she started. Her stomach lurched in arousal. All of this was so unfamiliar, yet with every second, fear edged further out of reach.

"Let me touch your breasts," he murmured.

"Aye, please..." It was difficult to speak over the mad gallop of her heart. Anticipation seethed inside her like a wild Highland storm. Her flesh swelled with longing, as if he already put his hands on her.

Will stepped back and cupped her bosom in gentle hands, squeezing until she was shaking. When his thumbs brushed the peaks through her transparent shift, the charge of sensation made her cry out.

"That's...that's wicked," she sighed, angling forward to encourage him.

"But nice?"

"Definitely nice."

When he bent to take one nipple between his lips, an even more powerful surge of arousal overtook her. While his hand toyed with her other breast, he drew on the beaded tip.

Ellen buried her hands in his hair to keep her balance, making a silent plea for him not to stop. In all her sheltered life, she'd never felt anything so marvelous as Will's lips on her breast.

Except perhaps his kisses. It was difficult to think of anything better than his kisses.

Her heart raced, and she had trouble taking in enough air to fill her lungs. Already she felt overcome, although despite her innocence, she recognized that they'd just started. The thought was both daunting and thrilling.

At the point where she wasn't sure whether she could endure more and remain upright, he raised his head. His gaze burned like flame. She moved to ease the weight in the pit of her stomach. Heaven help her, she was in such a state that even a look from him made her mad.

"May I take off your shift?" His guttural purr set her very bones vibrating.

She studied his features, reading desire and more dangerous for her sanity, something that looked like affection. "Do ye always ask permission?"

That fascinating mouth quirked. It was even more fascinating now, because she knew how it tasted. "Of course no'."

He caught her face between his hands. This time, she wriggled for a different reason. The piercing honesty of Will's stare left her nowhere to hide. His candid gaze swept away all defenses.

What then remained to her?

Ellen feared the answer to that question. But she'd wandered too far down the path of pleasure to save herself.

"I want ye to ken that you're in charge."

She'd seen enough to realize that playing second fiddle wasn't his style. "Ye like to call the tune."

"If I can."

"No' this time?"

"I placed myself at your service."

"Is that difficult?"

"I'll survive." Another self-derisive twist of his lips. "There are compensations."

"I suppose when you're with a lassie, ye usually know that she'll give you what you want."

"A man lives in hope."

For a fleeting instant, she wondered if he hoped for the same from her, but however heady the pleasure, she couldn't ignore her untenable situation. No matter how much she wanted to give herself to Will, she'd never risk conceiving a child. "I suspect those girls didn't say no."

Thick auburn lashes veiled his gleaming eyes. "A gentleman never tells."

Her short laugh surprised her. She hadn't expected his dry humor to leaven the intensity. "Aye, ye may remove my shift."

"Thank you, Miss Cameron."

As he tugged the shift over her head, the gentle mockery had her smiling. The room was warm, so nerves alone made a cold breeze whistle around her.

Ellen waited in an agony of suspense for Will to take her in his arms. She wished to Hades he would. Thought shifted out of reach when he kissed her, and she felt so devilish self-conscious, standing here without a stitch to cover her.

Her hands moved to shield her sex before she forced them back to her sides, closing them into fists. She trembled like a bird in a winter gale, and apprehension made her mouth as dry as dust. Apprehension and excitement. Because despite fear and embarrassment, it was thrilling to stand naked before this man she wanted so very much.

She summoned every ounce of courage to meet his eyes. "Say...say something," she forced out through a tight throat.

"You're so bonny, ye steal the words right away."

Astonishment thundered through her, left her floundering. This was a man with a smooth tongue. She'd noticed that from the first. Even come to appreciate it. But as she took in the raw emotion in his expression and heard it scrape in that deep voice, she realized that the sight of her body had struck this sophisticated man dumb.

How...marvelous.

Most of her life, she'd felt inadequate. Given she lacked the basic grace of a whole body, the name Fair Ellen had always seemed a snide joke. But as Will's gaze ranged over her nakedness with an awe that she couldn't mistake, she felt beautiful. New and unfamiliar confidence seeped through her, and her stiffness ebbed. She sucked in a ragged breath as her fingers slowly straightened.

Ellen wasn't sure who moved first. Perhaps they moved together. But on a soft sigh of anticipation, she found herself lashed to Will's tall form.

CHAPTER ELEVEN

Will drowned in Ellen's eager kisses, even as the image of her magnificent body burned against his eyelids. The milk-white skin, the tumble of golden hair, the rose-pink nipples crowning round, high breasts. The graceful lines of her arms and waist, and the hips full of womanly promise. The soft plain of her pale belly, above the sweet nest of dark blond curls at the delta of her slender thighs.

What a delightful mixture of shyness and boldness she was.

At the sight of her nakedness, he became as hard and ready as a stallion with a mare, God save him. No surprise there.

But the most powerful element wasn't his raging desire, mighty as that was. What ripped a chasm in his heart and left him floundering was the weight of emotion powering every second. Something beyond the profane elevated this encounter in a way he couldn't explain, something that beggared even his rich experience. It made him feel like a rank beginner, in a way he hadn't felt since...

Damn it, since he was a rank beginner.

Thank heaven, he wasn't a beginner, and he knew how to summon the magic slumbering inside Ellen's slender body.

By the time he lifted his head, she sagged in his arms, as if standing proved a challenge. He adored her wholehearted yielding. When she raised heavy eyelids, her dilated pupils were pools of darkness in a narrow circle of ice blue. Her eyes held a universe of sensual mystery.

"What ye do to me," she murmured.

What she did to him. Will reminded himself to rein in his impulse to lay her on the elaborate bed and bury his aching cock between her thighs. He'd made promises. He meant to keep them, even if it killed him.

Which was a possibility, given the agony in his balls.

Ellen gasped with surprise when he lifted her in his arms and carried her toward the bed, juggling her for a breathless moment as he swept back the covers. There was something fiendishly erotic in knowing that he was the only man who had ever shared this bed with her.

Erotic and moving, as so much about this slow, purposeful seduction proved moving. His hands were gentle as he set her upon the sheets. Instead of following her down, he took a moment to fan out that opulent mane around her exquisite face. A face stark with a longing that echoed the longing he felt for her.

"You're so beautiful," he whispered, as if he set foot inside a holy place.

The joy in her smile made his heart skip a beat. She didn't need to tell him that joy was no frequent visitor to her life. "When ye say that, I believe it."

Anger spiked for that thoughtless brute, her father, and that spiteful witch, her stepmother, and every other half-witted denizen of Inchgallen. Then he dismissed all thought of them. This wasn't the occasion to dwell on bitterness. This was the occasion for delight and discovery and happiness. "Ye should always believe it."

Poignant emotion tinged her smile. "I will."

He kissed her with more tenderness than passion, although passion massed inside him like a gathering storm. Her lips were soft and seemed to make vows of forever that she wasn't yet ready to speak in words.

When he raised his head, she slid across the bed and extended her arm toward him. "Come to me."

Will needed no further invitation. He settled beside her, rising on one elbow so he could watch her face. "Some of what I do might seem strange."

Her lips twitched with the humor that he'd always liked. It wasn't just her delicate beauty that attracted him. What he felt for Ellen went beyond shallow physical appeal.

Shallow physical appeal? Right now, the demands of his body felt more powerful than an earthquake. Shallow didn't even begin to describe this soul-deep craving.

"I'm sure it will."

"I'll go slowly."

"I'm no' sure I'll survive slowly."

Will wasn't sure he'd survive slowly either. "It's all part of the torture."

Her choked laugh sounded like anticipation. He kissed her and stroked her body. He trailed his fingers down her throat to find the frantic hammer of her pulse at the base.

She whimpered and squirmed against the sheets. "When ye touch me there, it makes me feel all wild and wanton."

"That's excellent."

"It's alarming."

He smiled. "Och, away with ye. Nothing alarms you, even a man climbing through your window in the middle of a tempest."

Ellen caught his hand and brought it to her lips. Gratification shuddered through him. So far, she'd proven an ardent partner, but she'd been too reticent to take the initiative. He wanted to lure her into playing his equal in pleasure. "I was alarmed."

"You didnae look it. I thought I'd end up taking a bullet."

"What a dreadful waste of a handsome Highland laddie."

He kissed her. "I'm very glad ye didnae shoot me."

Amusement lit her remarkable eyes. "At this moment, so am I."

His hand traced the line of her collarbone and ventured down the slope of her breast. This was torture, but he found delight in taking his time, too. Arousal added spice to his tender curiosity. There were rewards in savoring each moment, stringing them together like perfect pearls on a thread.

Ellen's skin was so fine-grained, it felt like silk beneath his seeking fingers. Her lavender scent was the air he breathed. He loved how what he did to her proceeded to a ragged rhythm of gasps and sighs.

He fondled her breast and toyed with a nipple that hardened against his palm. Her cracked exhalation told him that any remaining fears ebbed.

Will took her nipple between his lips, drawing on it until she quivered. His thumbnail scraped the other nipple, and she jerked in reaction before she raked her fingers through his hair in wordless encouragement to continue.

He lingered over her breasts, kissing each in turn, learning the honeyed taste of her skin. With gradual daring, still teasing her nipple with tongue and teeth, he slid his hand lower, spreading it across her stomach and dipping into the sweet indentation of her navel.

As she writhed, a shaky exhalation of laughter escaped. "That tickles."

He smiled against her breast then kissed the places his hands had just claimed. When she parted her legs, the rich scent of her excitement made his nostrils flare.

As he combed his fingers through the soft curls covering her mound, he took her lips with fierce hunger. The feathery hair was damp under his hand. Her thighs loosened, but still he tantalized her. And himself. A seduction by inches might risk ripping him apart, but it was working.

He slipped his hand between her legs. When he stroked the slick folds for the first time, she cried out against his lips and caught his wrist. "That's...that's depraved."

He smiled as he lifted his hand from her sex, giving her a chance to accustom herself to the idea of him invading her secret places.

"Aye, that it is. Let me show you how depraved."

An uncertain gaze searched his face for reassurance. Her reaction reminded him again that he needed to take care. The trust Ellen placed in him was a gift, but it was also an enormous responsibility.

Something in his expression must have soothed her fears, because the desperate grip on his arm eased. She ran her hand up his arm in a caress that had his heart crashing so hard against his ribs that he feared it must break free. "I'm being a henwit."

He dipped his head to kiss her. "You'll like this, my darling henwit."

"I have nae doubt I will." Wry amusement curled her lips. "I've liked everything else you've done."

"And we've hardly started."

Her eyes went round with shock. "The mind boggles."

He laughed and kissed her again, taking his time until she lay relaxed under the hand he rested on her midriff.

This time when he touched her, she murmured her approval and her legs eased open to permit him access. Satisfaction surged through him at her willingness.

He traced the delicate petals of her sex, relishing her satiny heat. She shifted, and her sigh this time conveyed pleasure.

When he found that secret pearl of flesh, she stiffened. Her breath emerged in panting gasps, and astonishment turned her eyes glassy. "Will, that's..."

He waited for some protest.

She bit her lip and angled higher. "That's wonderful."

He growled in agreement and concentrated on pleasing her. As she arched up, female excitement bathed his hand. "What on earth..."

Her frank surprise drew another choked laugh from him. "I'm going to put my finger inside ye," he said softly.

"Will it hurt?"

"I'll be gentle."

In a silent act of trust, she spread her legs wider. Her hand drifted down to rest on his bare chest. Her touch sizzled through him, and made his cock swell against his kilt. The soft wool over his throbbing hardness was a reminder to maintain control, even as control became more excruciating by the second.

He stroked her until she trembled. Carefully he slid his index finger inside her. She made an incoherent sound but didn't pull away.

"Are ye all right?" He watched her face for signs of discomfort. Despite her tightness, what he read in her eyes was burning curiosity. How he adored her daring.

"It feels odd, but it doesnae hurt."

"Good," he said, although touching her where he so wanted to put his cock made talking an almighty effort.

Will withdrew his finger then pushed it inside her again, feeling her resistance. Then when she shifted, he sensed a slight easing.

Ellen's hand flattened against his chest, and he felt the sting of her fingernails. He worked her until her body welcomed his invasion. She was shaking, and she tilted her head back against the pillows as she dragged air into her lungs. With her eyes closed, she looked like she strove after the unattainable. Her soft mews of pleasure were music in his ears.

This time, he placed two fingers inside her and curled them against her inner walls. She opened startled eyes and pushed her hips up. He kissed her, as he built a relentless rhythm. When she strained for her peak, he pressed his hand to her center of pleasure and watched in an agony of arousal as she crossed over.

Lost in the rapture of her first climax, Ellen was glorious. Will loved that he could do this for her.

Dazed blue eyes sought his, as she slumped against the sheets. "That was..."

When words failed her, she touched his face. The tender gesture cut as deep as those moments when she'd shuddered under his caresses. His heart gave another of those disconcerting lurches, as if she took it in her slender hand and squeezed it.

She kept catching him on the raw. He'd imagined that he'd teach her about what a man and a woman did together. It turned out that he ventured into new territory, too.

"Thank you," she whispered.

He wanted to smile, but he was too moved. "There's more."

Her eyes rounded. "More?"

"Aye."

"Good heavens above."

CHAPTER TWELVE

Ellen called out Will's name in a hoarse voice as yet again the world flared into blinding light. Pleasure gushed through her veins, and she clung to the ecstatic peak as long as she could.

It felt like a long time later when she floated down from some mysterious place in the stars. It was an effort to open her eyes, they felt so heavy.

Will leaned on one elbow and watched her, his golden gaze hungry. His hand draped across her bare stomach with tender possession. Only a few days ago, she'd have resented that hint of ownership, but tonight it just seemed part of the powerful bond uniting them.

He'd promised to leave her a virgin, but with every touch, every spark of pleasure, she realized that while he might preserve her physical chastity, he stole more of her emotional innocence. Even more unexpected, she welcomed his claim on her. She'd been so lonely on her rocky island. With Will, she didn't feel lonely at all.

Which foretold a loneliness to beggar even her wretched experience, once he sailed away.

Because their time together was so short, she found the courage to slide her hand around the back of his neck and draw him down toward her. "Kiss me, Will."

Somewhere in these last days, she'd come to trust him. Her trust was a rare gift. Too many people had wronged Ellen for her to have any confidence in a promise. Yet she believed Will would keep his word. Because of that, a painful tightness inside her loosened and spread its wings. She felt ready to fly.

Ready to fly? His touch had already flung her into the core of the sun and back. The memory of those extraordinary moments when she'd lost contact with earth still shuddered through her.

She waited for one of his wild, passionate kisses. Already she knew that his kisses covered a delightful range, from a sweetness that made her toes curl, to a rapacity that should terrify her but that instead made her blood thunder.

Rather than hunger, she met soul-piercing tenderness. Much more dangerous than passion. Dangerous, when she struggled to remember that what they did was a once-in-a-lifetime experience and that he'd leave her on her island. Leave her with nothing to sustain the long years ahead, except memories of a man's touch, a man's smile, and a man's care for her.

Nothing but memories. And, she feared, a broken heart.

She thought that she'd learned the meaning of longing during her hours with Will Mackinnon. Grim foreboding grew that she'd discover the true meaning of longing, once she faced life without him.

Now when it was too late to save herself, Ellen recognized her peril.

Even knowing that, she was helpless to resist his kiss. She strained up against him and nipped and sucked at his lips and dared to slide her tongue into his mouth as she feasted on his sublime taste. Greedy hands ran over his arms and shoulders and chest. She was so new to this sensual world that she found his physical reality enthralling. The heat and smoothness of his skin, the smooth ball of a shoulder, the flex of a tendon under her palm. The soft prickle of hair on his chest and arms.

To think, she now had an inkling of what pleasure was. To think, she now knew how to lure and seduce with a kiss. Murmuring appreciation against his lips, she plunged seeking hands into that wealth of hair to bring him closer. Through the tenderness, she felt his rising need.

It seemed an eternity before they drew apart, gasping. She stared into eyes alight with desire. "Are ye ready for more?" he asked.

Anticipation ripped through her. "More? I'll be a quivering mess."

"Och, you're a doughty lassie." Ellen loved the way amusement lit his eyes. "You'll come through."

Her short laugh was self-deprecating. "I'm glad ye have such confidence in me."

His humor faded, replaced by something she couldn't entirely interpret but which made her heart turn over in her breast. Devil take him, he kept catching her out like this, trapping her in emotion that she was too afraid to acknowledge.

"I believe ye can do anything, Ellen."

Shocked, she stared into that striking face. Her heart gave another of those giddy wobbles. "I cannae dance. I cannae run. I cannae get off this island."

Will frowned. "You're braver than ye ken."

Heaven help her, she needed to back away from this cliff edge looming in front of her. If she peered too far over, she'd lose her balance and fall. For a few hours in this secret tower on a lost island, Will

Mackinnon almost convinced her that she was perfect. But they both knew that wasn't true.

His frown deepened. "Stop it."

"Stop what?" she stammered, her fingers pressing into his shoulders.

This...attraction or whatever it was that drew them together was a product of unique circumstances, a fragile plant that would thrive nowhere else but on rocky Bortha. In the light of life off the isle, Will would see her for the broken creature she was.

"Stop listening to your father in your head."

"How..."

Will went on before she could argue with his unwelcome perception. She wasn't sure that she wanted him to see her so clearly. He already wielded too much power.

"I can always tell. Ye get a look in your eyes, as if you're retreating behind a barrier where nobody can hurt you."

Her throat was so constricted that it was painful to squeeze out a reply. "I fear that ye might hurt me."

Fear? More than that. She knew that he would. He invited her into a radiant new world, but when the doors of paradise closed, exile would sting more than anything her clumsy idiot of a father had ever done.

She watched denial dull Will's bright gaze. "Ye still don't trust me?"

Ellen could say something about their short acquaintance, but they both knew that was only a lying excuse. "Of course I do. Look at where I am and what I'm doing."

He shook his head. "I want more."

"Why?"

To her surprise, he smiled. The upward kick of the corners of his lips made her light-headed with enchantment. She was in such trouble here, and it was too late to save herself. Will Mackinnon's glowing eyes and skillful hands trapped her, just as much as her father's repudiation trapped her on this island.

"The pity of it is I dinnae know. But nae woman has ever put me in a spin the way you have, Ellen Cameron."

She tunneled her fingers through his hair as to her surprise, she smiled back. What was the use of trying to protect herself? It had been too late the day she waved a gun at him and told him to get out. "I like that."

"I thought you might." His smile hinted at devilry. "Now let me put ye in a spin."

"Ye said there was more."

"There is, bonny lassie. Lie back and spread your legs."

She stretched out across the sheets, then gave a gasp as he caught her by the waist and arranged her until her legs flopped over the side of the bed.

"Will?" she asked on a rising note, as he rolled off the mattress to kneel between her parted knees. She struggled up onto her elbows so that she could look down the length of her naked body to meet his glittering eyes.

He dropped a kiss on the top of her thigh. "I said I'd shock ye."

"You...you do. Ye have already."

She was achingly conscious that he could see her sex. Even as she told herself that she'd forsaken modesty when she stood naked before him, this new intimacy seemed a step too far. A shaking hand reached down to cover her mound.

"I promised ye pleasure," he murmured, to her relief, looking at her face rather than...down there. "Let me show ye."

"You've given me pleasure." Ellen cursed the quaver in her voice. She sounded as if she was terrified, and while she might have her issues with Will's view of her as brave and daring, her soul expanded every time he said it.

"I want to give ye more."

"But ye can...see me." He'd touched her in ways that she'd never imagined in her wildest dreams, but nonetheless it seemed beyond shocking that she lay on brazen display.

"You're beautiful from head to toe, lassie. And everything in between." He kissed her again, this time on the soft flesh of her stomach. Her interior muscles contracted in response. How bizarre to be afraid and at the same time consumed with lecherous curiosity.

"Can we no' do what we did before?" she asked, wondering how she could sound so childish about such a blatantly adult activity.

Will kept smiling. "We could, but I promise you'll like what I've got planned."

"Ye want to look at me?"

"I do indeed."

"Yet ye keep yourself covered."

Self-mockery tinged the smile. "That's out of necessity."

God forgive her, she was avid to see his naked body. Now her eyes rounded in amazement. "Will it frighten me?"

When he burst into laughter, the note of fondness beneath his amusement stopped her prickling up. He moved along her body until he kissed her.

She tried to hold back. He was altogether too charming for his own good – and hers. But it was useless. One touch of those lips, and she was lost.

How did he do that? A simple kiss made her believe that they shared one soul.

He lifted his head to stare into her eyes. "What's under there might make ye a little nervous. At first anyway."

"I'm nervous now."

More fondness softened his features. "I know, sweetheart."

"Are ye...deformed?"

Another huff of amusement. "No' yet. But what we're doing tonight makes me fear for my health."

"Will..."

"I'm in agony wanting you, Ellen." He kissed her quickly. "The kilt reminds me that I swore to keep ye pure."

Realization sent the breath whooshing out of her lungs. She knew that he wanted her, but in her innocence, she hadn't counted what it cost him to hold back. "I didnae understand what I asked of you."

"It's a bargain I was willing to make."

Her chest started to hurt. Stupid girl, she'd forgotten to breathe. She sucked in some air, and her vision cleared. What she saw made her heart ache.

That striking face was drawn, and his eyes blazed. A flush marked the edge of his cheekbones, and he looked as if he clung to honor by mere fingertips.

When Ellen had agreed to this, she'd only thought of herself. That here was a chance to discover what other women felt with a lover. And more mortifying, that she'd have Will's complete attention. When she was with him, she felt like the Ellen he described. Beautiful. Free. Bold. That feeling was as addictive as his touch.

Now she saw that what he did came at a price. The man before her was in pain.

"I'm sorry."

"Dinnae be. I count it a privilege to show ye the delights of your body."

"What about your body?"

A dismissive grunt. "That's why the Good Lord invented kilts."

She couldn't help laughing. "I dinnae want ye to suffer."

He shook his head. "All in a good cause."

"It doesnae seem fair that you give me such pleasure when there's nothing in it for ye."

A teasing light brightened his eyes. "I wouldnae say that. I get to touch ye and kiss ye and watch ye climax. A banquet of rewards, in fact."

"But ye want more." It wasn't a question. "You're doing this for my benefit, no' your own."

"Ellen, if you're determined to see me as a saint, I willnae argue."

"A saint?" She laughed. "Perhaps no' quite that."

He kissed her until she stretched beneath him, boneless with surrender. "I'm feeling rather saintly, which isnae the thing at all. Will ye give me my way?"

"If...if it's what ye want." She felt like she signed her life over to him.

"It is."

Ellen read amusement in his eyes, but also a ferocious appetite whose extent she'd only just recognized. Delightful trepidation twined its way through her. "Then go ahead."

Will took his time, kissing a trail down her body, lingering at her breasts. By the time he kneeled between her thighs once more, she was shaking. This time she didn't hide herself. Instead she spread her legs to make room for him.

It still shocked her that he could see her private places, but she was happy to give him his way. Even if her cheeks were hotter than the fire crackling in the hearth.

For a long moment, nothing seemed to happen. She rose on her elbows again to check what he was doing.

Will was staring at her sex. When his nostrils flared, she realized that he inhaled the scent of her arousal. Another voluptuous shiver rushed through her.

Then to her disbelief, she watched him dip his head. For an extraordinary moment, she felt the warmth of his breath. Then the wet heat of his mouth on her cleft.

"Will, you..." she choked out, burying trembling hands in his hair.

She tugged hard to pull him away. What he did was too sinful.

Instead of obeying the demands of her hands, he began to use his tongue, lapping at her with a sensual persistence that turned her blood to lava. Her frantic grip eased into a caress as response burgeoned like a towering wave.

Ellen now knew where this particular coiling suspense led. The spiraling sensation rose higher and higher and crested on a peak of luminous bliss. With a cry, she ceded to the insistent, blinding pleasure. By the time she descended from a fierce heaven that had her writhing on the sheets, Will was sitting up and watching her with intent eyes.

She raised an unsteady hand to wipe cheeks that were wet with tears. "That was extraordinary."

He smiled. "I hate to be smug..."

She smiled back, wondering if she'd ever find the strength to move again. "No, you don't. Ye love it."

He laughed and kissed her thigh. Her legs felt like wet string. The touch of his lips on her bare skin didn't help. "Ye could be right. Are ye sorry that I followed my inclinations?"

"Never."

Was that admiration in his eyes? Or something more profound?

Before Ellen could be sure, he rose to his feet. When her usually sure-footed lover stumbled, she felt rather smug, too.

He found his balance and lit a candle at the fireplace before he headed to the staircase. "Are ye hungry?"

For you.

She feared what her face might reveal, so she blinked up at the beams on the ceiling and realized that, yes, she was hungry. "Aye."

"I'll get us something to eat. Dinnae go away."

She liked his teasing. Nobody ever teased her. He made her feel part of the human race. She smiled toward the roof, in part at his joke, in part because her body felt weighted with pleasure. It took far too long to recognize that she was happy. "I willnae."

As she listened to Will run lightly down the stairs, she made a heroic effort not to dwell on the future. Instead, she let her pulse slow from its wild race, while she did her best to store every sensation in her memory. The night had been so crammed with new experiences, she feared that she might forget some detail.

Ellen waited in increasing impatience for Will to return. For pity's sake, what was he doing down there? Preparing a state banquet? She was too aware of time passing, when they had so little time. Once the wind died down, he'd sail away and never come back. Every minute with him was more valuable than rubies.

Those minutes ticked away one by one, while she lingered in her bedroom and he did whatever he did in the kitchen two floors below.

She left the bed, shrugging her peignoir over her nakedness. Although she had no more secrets from Will when it came to what her body looked like. Heat pricked her cheeks, as she recalled the slide of his tongue along her cleft.

She added peat to the fire and stoked it to a blaze. It might be summer, but a stormy night in the Hebrides was always cold. Then she lit her candle.

With more care than he had – an unwelcome reminder of her infirmity – she made her way downstairs. The wind was howling as if it wanted to level the isolated tower. She hardly heard it.

Once she reached the top of the last flight of steps before the kitchen, she blew out her candle. Will must have lit a couple of lamps, because she could see her way.

Ellen frowned as she descended. She could hear a rhythmic grunting. What on earth was wrong with Will? Was he sick?

Lost in the shadows, she poised on the last step and surveyed the room. On the table sat a tray with a plate of oatcakes and cheese and a full decanter and glasses. Will was in a chair before the fire, in profile to her.

Ellen needed a moment to realize what he was doing.

The unfastened kilt draped to the floor, and his long legs sprawled across the flagstones. His fist closed hard around his rod, moving up and down with a violent speed that made the breath catch in her throat. His head tilted back, and his Adam's apple protruded from his powerful throat. His lips stretched over his teeth, and his ragged breath emerged in time with his sliding hand. The other hand clutched the arm of the oak chair so hard that his knuckles shone white in the flickering firelight. His eyes were closed, and his skin clung tight to his arresting bone structure. He looked as if he fought a mighty enemy.

She must have made some smothered sound, although she meant to stay quiet and leave him some privacy. Despite her innocence, she understood that he had no intention of sharing this moment with an observer.

He froze into motionlessness and opened his eyes. With a slow turn of his head, he looked in her direction. Even at this distance, she read how blank and lightless his gaze was. What he was doing didn't seem to give him joy.

"Ellen..." he said in a choked voice, shamed color flooding his features. His hand went still, but he didn't lift it away from his rod.

She swallowed to ease a parched throat. On unsteady legs, she descended to the kitchen floor. "Ye were so long, I wondered what you were doing."

A grim smile lengthened his lips. "After what happened upstairs, I didnae trust myself to keep my word. I thought that if I took the edge off..."

"So this is for me?"

He shrugged, although the tension in his lean frame remained visible. "If ye like."

Wondering where her boldness came from, she ventured closer. "Then perhaps ye should let me help."

CHAPTER THIRTEEN

When Will heard that muffled gasp, he lifted his head. All eyes and ashen shock, Ellen hovered a few feet away, watching his lonely efforts at relief. Humiliation twisted his gut into knots. How he must disgust her.

He drowned in a mire of embarrassment as he waited for her to run away, but to his surprise, she stepped toward him. What she said hardly penetrated the blood thundering in his ears and the nausea churning in his stomach.

"What?" It emerged sharper than he intended, but, for pity's sake, could a man be caught in a less dignified moment?

Licking her lips, she braved another step closer. Her face was as red now as he was sure his was. He braced for disdain or even worse, horror, at his rough, masculine needs. Her gaze fastened on the hand clasping his erect prick, and she licked her lips again.

She took so long to answer that he feared the delay turned his hair gray. She fiddled with the sash tying her velvet robe. Will bit back a groan, only too aware that she was naked beneath the covering.

"You've given me so much tonight. I'd like to give something back to ye."

He surveyed her in disbelief. "You're no' revolted to find me here like this?"

She shook her head, sending that curtain of gold hair drifting around her. "No." She paused, then spoke in an even lower voice, so he had to strain to hear her over the crackle of the fire and the constant wail of the wind. "I'm fascinated."

His hand dropped away from his cock, as he stared at her openmouthed. "Ellen..."

She made an eloquent gesture. "I've been curious, as well, Will. Curious about how ye look without your clothes. Curious about what it would be like to touch you. Curious about...whether I can make ye feel a fraction as good as you make me feel."

He was thunderstruck. "I'm no' worthy of you."

She smiled. She no longer looked so shocked, although those beautiful blue eyes remained focused between his legs. His dick twitched in response, as he couldn't help imagining her hands closing around him. His imagination strayed toward her lips servicing him there, but surely that would be too much, even for a brave creature like Ellen.

After all, she was an innocent. Hell, before last night, she'd never even kissed a man.

"Of course ye are. You're the best of men, Will Mackinnon."

He found himself smiling back, although he was almost as hard and aching as he'd been when he'd fled downstairs. He'd been desperate to ease the agony in his balls, afraid that if he didn't, he'd lose himself in her presence. "Are we about to have an argument about which of us is the more deserving?"

"I ken what I'd rather do."

"What's that?" Although by now, he had a fair idea.

Glowing azure eyes locked with his, and at last he read the avidity in her face. She wasn't doing this as a reluctant return for the pleasure he'd shown her. She was doing this because she craved him. "I want to touch ye, Will. I want to discover what you like a woman to do to you. I want ye to shake under my hands the way you've made me shake. Please dinnae deny me."

Deny her? He felt like he'd knocked on the gates of heaven and they'd opened wide. He extended a hand in her direction. "Come here."

She moved swiftly and accepted his hand before settling on her knees between his splayed thighs. When her attention returned to his dick, it jerked in excitement.

If her eyes could do that, heaven help him when she touched him. He'd spill at the first brush of those slender fingers.

He released her and curled his hands around the oak armrests. "Do I frighten ye?"

She licked her lips again with an innocent greed that turned his blood to steam. "A wee bit."

Her honesty was part of her bravery. "You've never seen a naked man?"

To his surprise, her eyelashes fluttered down and color tinged her cheeks. "I've caught the guards swimming once or twice."

"Brazen hussy," he said in a fond voice.

Discomfiture tinged her short laugh. "Aye, but it's a very small island, ye ken?"

"I do indeed. Did ye want to touch them, too?"

Her eyes flashed up to meet his. "No!" She paused. "Anyway, none of them were nearly as...impressive as ye are."

He cupped her delicate jaw, loving the way she nestled her cheek into his palm. A tempest of sexual need rose around them, but tenderness hovered, as well, charging all that heat with radiance. "That's what a laddie likes to hear."

Her lips pursed. "You ken this was after my father placed his ban on young, handsome guards."

Will gave a theatrical sigh. "So you're saying I shouldnae be too flattered?"

She arched her eyebrows. "I'm sure even the young, handsome guards could never match up to ye, my fine Mr. Mackinnon."

"Och, that's better." Loving her teasing, he leaned in and kissed her.

When she pulled away, her eyes glowed with pleasure. "Anyway, their...things didnae look like yours."

He glanced down to where his prick rose hard and insistent. "After a dip in that cold sea, I'm no' surprised."

"May I...may I touch ye?"

"I'd like that more than anything."

Which wasn't completely true. What he'd like above all things would be to haul this lovely woman beneath him and plunge deep inside her.

Uncertainty shadowed her eyes. Had he ever been so aware of another person's reactions as he was of Fair Ellen's?

He'd led a blessed life. Since meeting Ellen, he'd never been so conscious of that.

But even discounting the danger that threatened them, with her father's men only a few miles across the sea, there was a piquancy to what happened with her that he'd never experienced. These last days had sloughed away a layer of insulation between him and life. In her company, everything seemed fresher, sharper, more poignant, more beautiful.

Their attraction had blossomed so fast, he needed to catch up with its full meaning. But he already knew that if he left Bortha without this bonny woman, life would lose all its color.

She was thinking on a more profane plane. "Will ye tell me what to do?"

"Let's see how ye manage on your own." She'd already proven herself such an inventive partner that he was curious to discover what she'd do, given free range of his body.

"I dinnae want to hurt you."

He snorted with grim amusement. "I ache for ye already."

"You didnae look like you were enjoying yourself when I found ye."

"I'll enjoy what ye do."

And also suffer. He accepted that. But he wanted those neat, deft hands on his body more than he wanted his next breath.

Her lips quirked. "I hope so."

He stretched out in his chair, extending his legs on either side of her so his feet rested on the mat in front of the fire. "I'm all yours."

Will sounded like he was joking, but he'd never meant three words more. Closing his eyes, he angled his head back. He braced for what he already knew was going to be agonizing delight.

She gave a shaky inhalation, and he could picture her serious expression. He didn't look at her, because he had a notion she'd feel less self-conscious without him watching.

So he jerked in surprise when she laid her hand on his bare chest. He should have known that she'd need to work her way up – or down – to touching his cock. The reminder of her innocence had his heart cramping.

As she rose over him, she slid against his bare thighs. In his agitated state, the soft friction of her velvet robe on his skin nearly blew the top of his head off. He felt the silky tumble of her hair as she bent to kiss an incendiary path across his pectorals then down his breastbone. More blasts of sensation.

By the time she traced her way across his belly, he was gasping and in danger of losing himself. She hadn't even taken him in her hand yet.

Just as stirring was the symphony of her enjoyment. Little hums and murmurs that expressed female appreciation. She'd learned a lot in the last hours, imitating what he'd done to her and adding something of her own to the heady mix. She drove him to the edge with a flick of her tongue or scrape of her teeth, and every so often a sharp little nip that smashed through him like cannon fire.

When he trembled on the brink, she lifted her head. The cessation in contact left him shaking and needy. For a long time, he remained unmoving, as he waited for her to touch him again.

Nothing.

All he could hear through the pulsing in his ears was the crackle of the fire and the erratic rasp of his breathing.

He opened dazed eyes just in time to watch her shape a trembling hand around his prick.

Lord Almighty! As heat encompassed him, he gritted his teeth until they threatened to crack. His muscles tightened to rock while he battled for control.

For most of the night, he'd been as hard as an iron bar. The ache in his balls had been unremitting. Now when Ellen fondled him, the urge for release verged on invincible. But he ground his teeth together and somehow held back, although every inch of him screamed at the cruel restraint.

He must have made some sound of discomfort, because she released him. "I'm sorry."

Will sucked air across a throat that felt like it was lined with gravel. "What the devil are ye doing?"

She shot him a troubled glance. "I knew I'd do it wrong."

"The only thing ye did wrong…"

"Aye?"

"Was to stop."

Her eyes widened. The lamplight revealed a return of the confidence that she'd started to find upstairs. "What are ye saying?"

He groaned. "Damn it, keep going, lassie."

"But ye sound as if I'm torturing you."

He wanted to laugh at her bewilderment, but he was too close to the brink. "It's torture to control myself." He started to sound more like himself, although his grip on the arms of the chair threatened to reduce that fine old oak to a pile of splinters. "But the Mackinnons breed braw warriors."

Her attention swept from his head to his toes then back again before settling on his throbbing dick. "Och, they most certainly do."

That comprehensive inspection claimed him. He'd never thought of wanting a woman to possess his heart and soul. It turned out that he wanted Fair Ellen to take everything he was and keep it safe forever.

Still she didn't touch him. Waiting for her next move – and her next move might be to stand up and march away up the stairs – was like being stretched on the rack. His torment mounted as those full pink lips curved up in a slow smile that he could only describe as gloating.

"You're at my mercy."

His groan came from the depths. "Nae need to sound so pleased about it."

"But I am pleased."

She didn't need to tell him that. "Ye enjoy torturing me."

"Of course." She kept smiling. "You've tortured me all night. It's nice to return the favor."

"Och, do your worst."

"Ye may have to help me learn how to touch you."

"It's a promise." Demand roughened his voice. "Now, for God's sake, Ellen, go back to what ye were doing. Or else I fear I'll explode into a thousand smoking pieces."

She had no trouble laughing, but then she wasn't poised on a knife edge of desperation. "Poor you."

He released a theatrical sigh, although his need was real. "If ye had a heart, you'd rush to ease my suffering."

She surged up over him and kissed him with clumsy enthusiasm. Just as the kiss took fire, she lifted away and fitted her hand around his cock again.

A tidal wave of heat engulfed him. Will tightened his grip on the chair arms until his hands ached. "Aye, that's it."

She firmed her hold. "Like this?"

"Move...move your fist up and down," he grated out.

"The way ye touched yourself?"

"Like that."

She followed his instructions, until his heart crashed against his ribs. "You're so big," she said in soft wonder, as he turned harder by the second. "I had nae idea."

His jaw came close to breaking under the pressure, as he bore the exquisite torment of her caresses. "More."

Through the pounding demand of his body, he remained conscious that this was Ellen who touched him. He'd never been so aware of his own responses. Yet despite his overwhelming need, he never lost sight of her lovely face.

She increased the pressure to a point where he felt he must shatter, before she paused to brush a drop of moisture from the tip with her thumb. Then the world dissolved into smoke when she bent her ruffled gold head and placed a tender kiss on the top of his dick. The soft movement of her lips was too much for his shredding control.

"Ellen..." He released the chair and lunged forward to push her down onto the worn rug in front of the fire.

She went willingly, although a cry of shock escaped her when he shoved aside the loose robe. Her shaking hands caught his arms in a frantic hold, as he spilled himself in gasping ecstasy on her bare stomach.

CHAPTER FOURTEEN

Will stirred in the big bed, not sure what had disturbed him. He was sleepy and content in a way he hadn't been in days. Ellen lay naked in his arms, cuddled up to his side as if she couldn't bear being more than an inch away. Her breasts pressed soft and warm into his side.

He angled his head to stare down into her face. He'd always thought her beautiful. How could he think anything else? But after the joy they'd found through the night just past, he saw that she was lovely right to the bone.

Her generosity left him in awe. More than that, she'd met him as an equal, every step of the way. Brave, spirited, giving. She was a woman in a million. He wanted to go on his knees to his Maker and thank him for this treasure, hidden on the far edges of the Hebrides.

Except lying here with his lover was so delightful that he had no intention of shifting.

Despite everything that they'd done to each other, he'd kept his promise and she remained a virgin, if not near as innocent as she had been. He found that almost impossible to believe. They'd veered excruciatingly close to consummation so many times, but he'd managed to control his impulses. Heaven knew how.

Even at the extreme limits of desire, he'd never forgotten what trust she'd placed in him.

In the dim light of the shuttered room, those delicate features snatched anew at his heart. She looked exhausted, thoroughly tousled. Happy. Her hair was a tangled skein of gold, and pink marked her skin where his beard had caught her.

It wasn't long since they'd collapsed exhausted onto the bed. After that unforgettable encounter in front of the kitchen fire, she'd brought him to climax again. That time, she used what she'd learned from her first attempt to tease him to insanity.

He'd wondered if his needy, gasping release might repulse her. It was why he'd left her alone upstairs while he escaped to find relief. Will should have known better. His darling might look like she dwelled in ethereal realms, but what they'd done proved that she relished earthier pleasures. He'd soon realized that touching him excited her.

Twice more, he'd used his hands and his mouth to bring her to her peak. By the last time, she was so weary that the climax washed over her like a soft warm ocean.

After the passion, he'd kissed her softly. Tenderness lingered as she moved her mouth against his with a sweetness that turned his blood to warm syrup.

Somewhere in the wee small hours, he'd bathed her. Then she'd returned the favor. Washing the traces of the long night from her slender body felt like a holy act. Odd that their carnal experiments resulted in reverence. He'd never felt that with a lover before.

Also bizarre that this night with Ellen should be the most intimate experience of his life. A night when the final intimacy hadn't taken place. He felt closer to this woman than he ever had to any mistress.

Even now, when he had a cock-stand of epic proportions, it was enough to lie beside her in this rumpled bed and watch her sleep. Early morning stillness wrapped around him like an embrace.

Early morning stillness...

Hell and damnation. What the deuce was he doing?

Now he knew what had woken him. The wind howling around Ellen's tower had become part of his world, the counterpoint to every minute he spent on Bortha.

This morning, all he could hear were gulls and blackbirds and the crash of waves below the cliff. The gale might have passed, but the sea remained rough.

The wild wind had kept him and Ellen safe. Its departure promised disaster.

Yet only with the greatest reluctance did he bend his head to kiss Ellen's disheveled golden crown. He tightened his hold. For one last moment, he pretended that they had all the time in the world to discover each other.

With a sleepy murmur, she kissed his chest, although she wasn't yet awake. He inhaled her warm floral scent. "Ellen, my darling, wake up."

She shifted again. The slide of her body sent arousal crashing through him, and he pictured how they might have filled the day.

Then he pushed away all thoughts of languorous hours here in Ellen's luxurious bedroom. He drew her up and kissed her. How he wished that they had more time. But wishes were dangerous now.

Her lips moved beneath his and when he raised his head, she was awake. He stared into misty blue eyes as she gave him a smile that wordlessly conveyed her delight in him.

"Good morrow, Will," she said, her voice hoarse with sleep.

"Good morrow, *mo chridhe*."

She frowned to hear him call her his heart. He kissed her again to cut off the inevitable protest. She curved into him with a readiness that did nothing to bolster his restraint. He'd risen over her and started to caress her breast before he recalled the looming threat. It was early, only just past five on the ormolu clock, but every minute counted.

He made an almighty effort and pulled free. Her disappointed sigh almost made him kiss her again. But that was the path of madness.

"Ellen, listen..."

"Aye?"

Despite his worry, he couldn't help smiling. "No, my bonny, *listen*."

Another frown contracted her fine dark gold eyebrows. "But I dinnae hear anything."

"Exactly."

Will watched fear replace melting surrender. He hated that change. Even more, he hated what followed. A devastation so stark, it threatened to break his heart.

She sat up and caught him by the shoulders, hands frantic instead of caressing. She reminded him of the determined lady who had threatened to shoot him. Was that only three days ago? It felt like a lifetime. He was no longer that brash, shallow man. Fair Ellen had turned him into a new and better version of himself.

"Will, for the love of heaven, why do ye delay? You're in mortal danger. My father will send the guards over, the moment they can launch a boat."

"Ellen, I cannae go like this."

"Aye, you can. You must." Her voice vibrated with urgency. "I willnae live with the idea that I brought harm to ye. If my father's men find you, they'll kill you."

His jaw set firm. "I'm well able to defend myself, lassie."

She shook her head, as pale and desperate as last night she'd been soft and rosy with female satisfaction. "I'm sure ye are, but I dinnae want my kinsmen murdered either. And my father will only send more men across."

"I dinnae want to leave ye."

"Dinnae make me watch you die." Eyes alight with terror fastened on his face. "I can bear to be lonely and alone, as long as I ken that you're alive somewhere."

He shrugged out of her hold and caught her hands, ignoring her struggles to pull away. "You dinnae have to be lonely and alone, Ellen. Ye can come with me."

CHAPTER FIFTEEN

Ellen was in such a lather to get Will away to safety that she didn't hear what he said. She fought to break free, having some idea that if she no longer touched him, he might heed her warnings. Perhaps if he'd seen the bloodshed when a few of the suitors came to grief, he'd understand her urgency. The thought of Will's vigor and intelligence and beauty sprawled lifeless on Bortha's rocky shore made her feel sick.

"Will, get dressed."

Still he didn't move. Still he didn't release her, curse him. "Ellen, did ye hear me?"

"I'll go and fix some food for your voyage."

"Ellen!" he said sharply.

Something in his tone penetrated her panic. "Aye, what is it?"

His grip firmed, and hazel eyes captured her gaze. "Come with me."

For a fleeting instant, her heart ceased its lunatic rush. The extravagant setting of her bedroom receded from sight. She beheld a golden, unfamiliar world where she wed Will Mackinnon and bore his children and accepted his attentions as her lifelong right, not as a brief oasis in a barren desert.

Then very deliberately, she put aside that unattainable dream and made herself concentrate on the here and now. It was the hardest thing that she'd ever done. Much harder than standing before him naked last night. She squashed down the anguish shredding her soul and raised her chin.

This time, when she tried to escape Will's hold, he let her go.

"Ye mean to refuse me." She'd never heard that rich baritone sound so flat.

"I do." The words sliced at her like razors.

"Why?"

Ellen scrambled out of bed to pick up her robe and shrug it over her nakedness. She needed armor against what she saw in his eyes. "Will, right now this isnae important."

"You're wrong." Blast him, instead of leaving the bed, he pushed himself higher against the stacked pillows. "It's the most important thing in the whole world."

The gallant fool. Couldn't he see that all that mattered was getting him off this island in one piece? "Just go."

He didn't shift. By heaven, he was a stubborn sod. "Tell me why you willnae come."

"Because I belong on Bortha."

"Horseshit."

She gasped at his bluntness. While she struggled to come up with a reason to convince him, she crossed to fling the shutters wide on the windows facing east. Danger would come from that direction.

The wide channel between Inchgallen and Bortha was choppy with waves and empty of boats. She sucked in her first proper breath since she'd realized that her time with Will reached its end.

When she turned to face him, she wished that she hadn't. He didn't look angry. He was a remarkably even-tempered man, which made a nice change from her father's tantrums. But she saw that he was determined to persuade her to follow his absurd suggestion. Worse, looking at him when he was so very dear to her just made her heart crave what it couldn't have.

"I've only known ye three days. You'll regret a sudden decision."

He looked unimpressed with that. She couldn't blame him. Their acquaintance might be short, but it had been intense. This sounded mad, but she knew Will Mackinnon better than she knew anyone on earth. She suspected that he knew her, too.

"It's no' a sudden decision." He remained calm. "I've asked ye before."

"That was just a trick to seduce me."

His gaze didn't waver. "Ye know better than that."

She did, God help her. Which didn't make it any easier to do the right thing.

Nor did his sheer magnificence as he lay stretched across the bed in unself-conscious nudity. To think, if she went with him, she could touch that superb body whenever she liked. She wouldn't have to starve to death on memories. Or torment herself, imagining him out in the great wide world, finding some other lady to take as his lover.

"We dinnae have time for this." The sea might be empty right now, but it wouldn't stay that way.

He remained where he was. "I'm offering ye a place of honor as my wife, Ellen. Do me the courtesy of telling me why you willnae accept it."

Will..." she whispered, tears pricking her eyes and hands clenching at her sides until her fingernails dug into her palms. The sting reminded her to be strong. For Will's sake more than her own.

But, oh, how she'd treasure this moment, as she dwindled away on this isolated rock. Once, once, a man she wanted more than life had asked her to marry him. That ember would lend a scrap of warmth to a cold, lonely future.

His eyes sharpened. "Do ye think I mean to steal you away and make you my mistress? You misjudge me, my lady."

Weariness, heavy as an anvil, descended. "What I think is that you've succumbed to all the romantic nonsense about Fair Ellen of the Isles. You see yourself as St. George, rescuing the maiden from the dragon and sweeping her away to find happily ever after. You've fallen victim to Highland mist and fantasy."

He'd gone pale, and a muscle flickered in his lean cheek. "So even after last night, you dinnae trust me."

"You're a good man, Will." Her gesture encompassed her entirety with all its glaring faults. Plague take him, why couldn't he see what was so obvious to her? "The fact that I'm a virgin this morning proves it."

"You dinnae want a good man?"

Oh, that hurt. That hurt like the devil.

Because if that good man was William Mackinnon of Achnasheen, she wanted him beyond bearing. But Will was lost in a fairy story, and she'd spent ten years on Bortha coming to terms with bleak reality. If she'd learned anything through all her travails, it was that bleak reality trumped pretty dreams every single time.

"I dinnae want a man who's caught up in a grand romantic story. Because he'll come back to earth with a nasty bump when he finds himself shackled to a crippled wife." She hoped the harsh description would wake Will up to the desolate truth.

"You judge me to be the same as your father?" His voice remained flat, but she saw that he battled with titanic emotion. "Unable to see your quality because ye walk a wee bit unevenly."

She shook her head, even as a bitter laugh escaped. "No, I honor your generosity. I honor your...honor. But ye need a woman to walk at your side, not limp a couple of yards behind you, always struggling to keep up."

A lacerating silence crashed down. Her longing eyes drank in every inch of him. Because while she'd never be a fitting wife for this wonderful man, nothing could stop her loving him. She wanted to imprint every detail on her memory, even now when he was angry and disappointed in her.

Ellen returned to the window and breathed a sigh of relief to see that the sea remained empty. When she turned back, Will stood beside the bed. He'd tugged on his kilt and a shirt hung loose about his narrow hips.

From several feet away, his eyes bored into hers. Could he see how she struggled to do right by him? Could he see how excruciating it was to deny him, when some weak and stupid part of her would love nothing better than to leave Bortha with him?

But she had too much pride to accept a husband who was so superior to her in every way that the world counted as important. The prospect of looking into Will's beloved face and reading regret for his choice was more than she could bear.

Ellen trusted Will enough to know that he'd never despise her weakness. But pity would be worse. If he ever pitied her, her soul would shrivel to ash. Yet what other end could she expect?

He stood straight and tall – another reminder of his physical splendor, should she need it. When she'd first met him, she'd dismissed him as nothing more than a handsome rogue, up for any dare that amused him. The man who stared her down was still handsome, so handsome he broke her heart. But now he looked like a carved effigy from one of her folios of etchings. Etchings of places she'd never see.

Will was stern and intent, and he appeared older than his twenty-eight years. "You're trapped here forever, then, Ellen," he said in a hard voice.

She was grateful that he didn't try to change her mind with pretty words and soft caresses. If he did, she couldn't be sure that she'd hold out.

"Of course I am."

"No' just your body, but your mind. You've taken yourself at your father's valuation, and that's placed chains around your heart and soul. It's a sodding tragedy."

She faltered back with a choked cry. "That's no' fair."

His expression didn't soften. Through all their time together, she'd basked in his smiles and his laughter and his care for her. This man looked like he faced down his greatest foe. "Is it no'?"

As she found her balance, she realized that she'd hurt him. He might be lost in an impractical dream of the two of them making a life together. But the flimsiness of his hopes didn't save him from genuine pain at her rejection. Remorse flooded her, even as she recognized that she couldn't succumb to it.

She squared her shoulders. "What we have on Bortha..."

"Has been a miracle."

His unexpected interruption made tears rush to her eyes. That was true for her, but it was a surprise to hear he felt the same. A surprise and a blow.

"I'm glad ye feel like that," she admitted, then cursed her concession when he stepped forward and extended his hand.

"It's spitting in fate's face, if ye make me leave without you."

"There ye go again, talking about things that don't exist." She tried to sound scornful, but her response emerged as a sigh, rather than a reprimand.

"I believe I found your island because I was meant to. I believe that we were born to be together." Fervor rang in his voice, as his hand dropped down to his side. "I believe that ye were created to be my wife and live at Achnasheen as the mother of my children."

"Oh, Will..." Tears overflowed. "I wish it was different."

"Ye can make it different," he said implacably. "It just takes determination and confidence that we can build on what we started here."

She raised shaking hands to dash the tears away, but more poured down to replace them. "You dinnae understand."

"Aye, I do. You're afraid to leave this island where you're safe and nobody is cruel to ye."

"I loathed being an object of derision in my father's house." She lifted her chin and tried to glare at him, but that proved impossible when her face was awash with tears. "You cannae blame me for no' wanting to endure that again."

"Nobody will disrespect ye in my presence. I can't see anyone of good heart wanting to anyway."

Her lips turned down. "But the world is full of bad people, Will. I dinnae want to be forever pointed out as the unfit wife of the resplendent Laird of Achnasheen."

"Ye make too much of your limp. I've reached a point where I hardly notice."

"Liar."

"I've never lied to ye, Ellen. You're a beautiful woman with a giving heart and a fine mind. If the world can't find enough in that to admire, it's the world's loss, no' yours."

"You're being kind again."

Will growled and scraped one hand through his hair, rumpling it. "No, I'm being honest. I dinnae want to go without you. The thought of leaving ye a prisoner on this island makes me sick to the stomach."

Ellen shook her head. "If I come with ye, I'll be your prisoner instead."

The remark hit its target and set that muscle dancing in his cheek once more. "I swear if I take ye off Bortha, I'll expect nothing from you. You're free."

Free to hanker after him or free to marry him, knowing that she did him a great wrong? Neither sounded very much like freedom to her.

She glanced out the window. Fear sharp as an ice pick carved a crevasse in her soul. That dark speck on the horizon could only be the boat from Inchgallen. She'd watched its approach often enough to recognize the shape of the sail, even from this distance. "Will, I see the boat. We've probably got an hour, but it's better if ye go now."

"But you willnae come with me."

She turned to catch a bewildered misery on his face that made her heart wither. "I belong on Bortha."

His hands spread in appeal. "Ye belong with me."

If only it were true.

Will went on in that same urgent voice. "I praise God and all his angels that I managed to catch ye when you were alone and unguarded. This time will never come again."

"No," she said, through lips that felt like wood. "It will never come again. Just as ye must never come here again."

His baffled anguish was such agony for her to see. "So you're happy for me to sail away today and for us never to see each other?"

She straightened shoulders that showed a lamentable tendency to slump. "My happiness has nothing to do with it."

"Your happiness should have everything to do with it, Ellen." Anger flashed in his eyes, turned them caramel. "Stop being so humble. Reach out and take what ye want."

If only she could. But she was too aware that in reaching out, she'd stumble. Will would catch her, she knew that to her bones. But the tragedy of it was that she didn't want him to carry her. She wanted to be his equal.

If she took what she wanted, in the end he'd feel sorry for her. In the end, he'd start to resent her. Proud Will Mackinnon was made to bestride the world, not wait in fuming impatience for his lame wife to catch up to him.

How her own pride balked at that idea.

She swallowed to ease her tight throat. And again, so she could speak the words that cut her like broken glass. "I told ye no. You must accept my decision."

His jaw set with a stubbornness that she'd never seen in him before. "And if I say I willnae go unless you come with me?"

That ice pick twisted in the wound, and for a moment everything went black.

"Ellen!"

A strong hand circled her arm and kept her upright. She sucked in a jagged breath to clear the horrific images from her head. "If ye die because of me, I'll never forgive myself. Or you."

"Ye can choose to escape from Bortha."

"This is the freedom ye offer, is it?" It took all her strength, but she straightened away from Will. "Emotional blackmail, so your wishes prevail over mine? I'd thought better of ye."

Shame shadowed his features. "I'm sorry."

Ellen unhooked his hand from her arm. She stepped away, in part because she didn't trust her resolve when she stood so close. "For God's sake, if ye have an ounce of care for me, please go now."

His face turned even more austere. The deep lines running between his nose and mouth betrayed how he fought to contain his dissatisfaction with her decision. "Ye leave me little choice."

Ellen sagged with relief, even as pain slashed at her. Because clinging to harsh reality was inhumanly difficult when her foolish, longing heart told her to take the chance, to go with Will. She stole another forbidden second to picture the life that she might have with him. This wonderful, gallant man at her side, children with his vivid red hair and flashing smile. Years together with Will, free of her father's poisonous influence.

The heroine in that particular story needed to be worthy of the hero. Ellen Cameron with her halting gait was no leading lady.

Fear overcame anguish. He might consider himself a match for any man, but her father's guards would overpower him with force of numbers, never mind how valiant a warrior he was. "You must go."

Will looked unreconciled with their parting. She couldn't help but find comfort in knowing that he was as reluctant to leave her as she was to send him away.

Ellen couldn't bear to stay and watch him prepare to leave. Every moment tempted her to toss good sense to the winds and beg him to take her with him. She turned and made her way downstairs as fast as her lame leg allowed.

By the time he appeared in the kitchen, she'd dragged on a blouse and kirtle from the clean laundry pile and tied her hair back in a rough plait. She'd pushed her feet into half boots. With shaking hands, she shoved a bundle of food and a flask of cold spring water into a leather satchel and extended it toward Will.

Her eyes stung with the tears that she refused to shed, but her voice was impressively steady as she spoke. "For your journey."

She wanted Will to remember her as brave and determined, not as a blubbering mess. Even if he must guess the effort that it took for her not to wail like a banshee at the prospect of losing him.

"Thank you," he said, sliding the satchel strap over one broad shoulder.

"You'll need to row to get out of the cove, but once you're in the open sea, ye can use your sail. Because you're leaving from the western side, with a bit of luck, they willnae see you." It was almost a relief to talk about practicalities. "I'll do my best to distract them and keep them down on the beach. They'll have supplies to unload before they start patrols."

"Are ye coming to the boat with me?"

"I'll slow ye up too much."

She waited for Will to argue, as he always did when she mentioned her infirmity. But despite sending her a sharp glance, he remained silent.

"Ye should go," she said after a thorny pause, wondering how she managed to put words together when she felt like she disintegrated in front of him. If she thought of what awaited her once he was gone, all she saw was desolation.

"Will ye walk me to the door?"

Ellen nodded and preceded him down the last flight of steps to the dark room where the guards lodged. They emerged into a day bright with sunshine. How she cursed the clement weather. How she cursed the fact that the storm hadn't lingered for another day.

Although parting from Will would be no less excruciating for being delayed.

Now, too late, she was agonizingly sorry that she'd placed any restrictions on what they'd done. Now, when regret bit deeper than a sword thrust, she wished that she'd been brave enough to accept Will's possession. She'd love to cling to the memory of his body moving inside hers. Even the thought of bearing his child didn't seem as terrifying as it once had.

"Is this really goodbye?" he asked.

She made herself meet that somber gaze and braced for a final farewell. "Aye."

I won't cry. I won't cry.

This one last time, she wanted to see him clearly. She wanted to note every detail, so that she never forgot a moment of what they'd done. Her hungry gaze took in the perfect bone structure, the glittering eyes, the expressive mouth, the tall, powerful body.

He was so beautiful. Right now, that struck her as cause for sorrow rather than rejoicing. As she drank in his physical allure, she had trouble believing that she'd spent all those sultry hours in his arms.

Yet she had, she had. Whatever misery he left behind, she couldn't regret one single minute of it.

"Kiss me, Ellen," he whispered, stepping closer.

For the last time.

How could she bear this grief? This separation ripped her to jagged, bleeding pieces.

"Aye," she said on a breath of sound. She put her arms around him and raised her face.

She waited for one of his gentle kisses, the ones that always threatened to crack her heart and now surely would. But his mouth was hungry and ruthless. His tongue penetrated deep and flickered against hers in an explosion of sensual intent. On a muffled sound of surprise, she kissed him back with all the passion that he'd awoken in her.

She gave a murmur of surrender as her hands rose with trembling eagerness to seize handfuls of his hair. Their affinity was more than carnal. She'd always known that. But after all they'd done to each other, this onslaught of physical pleasure was intoxicating.

When he lifted his head, she'd collapsed on his chest, unsure whether her knees would support her. Her blood pumped hot and hard, and she couldn't see straight. Her fingers tangled in his shirt, as if she tried to keep him with her.

She glanced up, almost afraid of what she'd see in his face. What she found sent fear slamming through her. Whether of Will, or of the arrival of her father's men, she couldn't say. His eyes bored down into hers as if her face was the only thing he saw. Heat more powerful than the sunlight radiated off him.

She gave herself a sharp reminder to send him away and fast. It was bad enough knowing that she'd never see him again, but the thought of him dead was unendurable.

Her command emerged low and urgent. "Ye must go, Will. The boat will be here soon."

"Aye, I'll go." He paused to suck in a deep breath. She watched his features harden with determination. "And so, my lady, will ye."

She frowned, too stirred up after that kiss to make sense of what he said. Then in a flash, she realized what he meant to do. With a broken cry, she whirled to run back into the tower. But as so often, her weak leg betrayed her.

Ellen stumbled on the step. Will seized her around the waist and flung her over his shoulder. She landed so hard that her breath escaped in an audible puff.

CHAPTER SIXTEEN

"Will, put me down," Ellen snapped. More than surprised, she was furious. He needed to escape, but he didn't need to cart her away, too, God rot him.

"No' on your life, my darling." At last, he started moving with the speed the situation warranted. "You're coming with me."

She knew that he wouldn't drop her. Even so, the ground below her moved at a dizzying rate, as he ran down the rocky slope toward the cove where his boat waited. She started to punch his back and kick. He grunted with discomfort and tightened his grip on her rump.

"Stop that, or you'll ruin our hopes of having children. Which would be an awfu' pity, when you'll make the bonniest mother in Scotland."

The laughter in his voice was the last straw. A growl exploded from deep in her throat. She redoubled her struggles, but neither her wriggling nor her curses made him pause. He turned his strength against her in a way he never had before.

"Let me go, ye great, hulking bully." In this position, talking was uncomfortable, but she was so het up, she managed it.

"No." Although he negotiated a steep hillside while he carried her, he didn't sound even a wee bit winded.

She gasped for air to fuel her tirade. "I'll never forgive ye for this."

His arm curved under her buttocks, using her skirt to restrict her kicking. She was sickly aware that her feeble fists made little impression on that powerful back. To think, she'd once gloried in his manly vigor. She'd had no idea what trouble she was getting into.

"I'm no' leaving you on this island to fade away. Or even worse, to fall prey to some unprincipled bastard who shows up with an army."

"Why should that be any worse than...what you're doing?" she asked in a choked voice, as angry, frightened tears rose. She tried closing her eyes, but that just made her nauseous.

"Don't be a silly widgeon, Ellen." They were nearly at the cove. "Of course it's better."

"Why? Because that paragon...Will Mackinnon does the kidnapping and no' some...unwashed ruffian?" Every time his feet hit the ground, he knocked the breath out of her, so her harangue emerged in jerky fragments.

Her biting sarcasm had no effect. Instead, the scoundrel had the temerity to chuckle. "Och, go on with ye, lassie. You ken in your heart you want to come with me."

Anger lent her a burst of energy. "Now ye can read my mind? Goodness me, you're a man among millions. And to think ye set your sights on poor little me."

Another short laugh. "By my faith, you've got a tongue on ye. When we're married, I'll have to watch my step."

"Plague take you, this isnae a joke, Will," she said in a cold tone. "If ye steal me away against…my wishes, you're as great a villain as any…of the men who came here before you."

"You dinnae believe that." His boots squeaked across damp white sand. She lay panting over his shoulder. So frustrating that all her struggles had got her precisely nowhere. But that didn't mean she gave up the fight. Far from it.

"Once more, you're able to read…my thoughts. Ye should go on…the stage. You'd make a fortune."

He responded with more of that annoying equanimity. "I can read your thoughts. Sometimes anyway. Ye can read mine, or guess at them. It's part of our closeness."

If she'd been standing upright and staring into his eyes, what he said might have made her melt. Slung across his shoulder like a sack of barley, she wasn't quite so ready to relent. "If I read your thoughts about disregarding my every wish, I'd have thrown ye out the day I saw you, my fine laddie."

"Och, give it a rest, Ellen." Will stopped beside the boat. It was pulled high up on the beach and stashed under a projecting shelf of rock, out of reach of the tide. "You're no' really that angry with me."

"There you're wrong, blast ye." Speech was becoming more difficult, with her stomach crushed against one sinewy shoulder. "I wish I had my pistol. I should have…followed my first impulse and shot…ye."

Will's long-suffering sigh only made her itch to clout him again. "Ye dinnae want to shoot me. We both know that. We also both know that ye want to come with me, and cowardice is all that's stopping you."

He accused her of being afraid? The prancing poltroon. She wasn't afraid of anything, including Will Mackinnon. "How dare you, ye..."

That calm, beautiful baritone spoke over her. "You're in love with me and cannae face the thought of a separation. But you've been stuck on this island so long on your own, you've convinced yourself that you're unfit for the world outside Bortha."

In love with him? He made a lot of cocksure claims, the devil. Rage rose so hard and high, she saw nothing but red. "Why, ye arrogant, misbegotten, vainglorious... Oof!"

With a bump, he set her on the wooden seat spanning the stern. Her feet splashed into the water in the bottom of the boat.

Again he spoke over her spluttering tirade. "Which is an altogether grand state of affairs, because I'm so in love with you that I cannae see straight."

"Nothing ye can do would..." Ellen stopped as what he'd said penetrated the fog of temper. "What did ye say?"

He smiled at her the way he'd smiled at her last night, as if he'd never beheld anything so splendid. "I said I love you."

Her answer emerged immediate and irrefutable. "You cannae."

Shaking his head, he replied with matching certainty. "Of course I can. But perhaps we should delay this argument until we're well away from your father's guards."

A reminder that right now Ellen had more to worry about than her aching heart. She raised shaking hands to her lips. "Ye have to go, Will."

"I do." He set the satchel beside her on the seat. "The question is – are ye coming with me?"

"Do I get a choice?"

"Of course ye do."

"Then why all the dramatics? Why hoist me around and haul me down here to get my feet wet?"

He glanced at the sloshing bilgewater. "Sorry about that."

"That's nae answer." She glanced around the debris-strewn beach and the rough sea. The sun might shine, but the recent stormy days had left their mark. Not least on her soul.

"You wouldnae listen to me up at the tower."

Her arms folded across her bosom and she glared at him, although it was hard to maintain her outrage. He'd spiked her guns the moment that he told her he loved her, even if she didn't yet concede the fight. "Who says I'm listening to ye now?"

"Och, you're listening, all right. What do ye say?"

The reality of what he'd said gradually seeped in, chasing away her anger, much as she wanted to cling to it as her only defense. Will must have noticed a softening in her tone, because the stiffness drained from his tall body. His hands spread to indicate that he'd been helpless to stop his heart opening to her.

How could she quarrel with that? Hadn't it been the same for her, right from the start? She wasn't quite ready to surrender, though. She needed to be sure.

One thing kept niggling. "You love me..."

Could this exceptional man love her? She thought back over their days together and remembered his care and consideration. And his passion. And how despite what it had cost him to hold back, she remained a virgin.

"How could I do anything else but fall in love with ye?"

"Because I'm the princess in the tower, waiting for her white knight to save her?"

His laugh was dismissive. "Don't be daft. I've never been a man to lose his heart to a legend. I lost my heart to a flesh and blood woman who makes me laugh and long and desire. I've fallen in love with ye, Ellen Cameron."

Somewhere in her essentially honest soul, she admitted that Will was right and she was afraid. What she was most afraid of was that he'd stop looking at her the way he was looking at her now. What if he ended up repenting that he'd invited a broken creature to share his life?

"I limp," she said in a flat attitude.

He shrugged. "Aye, ye do. Does that mean you're unworthy of happiness? Surely no'."

She twined her hands together and foolish tears misted her vision. "I'm reluctant to be a burden to ye."

His amusement faded, replaced by a serious expression that she'd never seen before. "You're no burden. You're a gift from heaven." He paused, but she was too overcome to answer. He went on. "I ken you're scared of what may happen to ye if you leave Bortha, and your pride smarts at the idea of people pitying your lameness. But I'm asking ye to conquer both fear and pride and come with me now. Because if you dinnae come, you'll break my heart. I love you, Ellen. I've never said that to another woman. Dinnae make me live without you. I couldnae bear it."

She blinked to clear the moisture from her eyes, as she strove to tell herself that she was the wrong woman for Will. That she was suited for life nowhere except Bortha. That she refused to put herself and her infirmity on show again.

But none of it mattered because of three words.

I love you.

And she, heaven help her, loved him. Would the pain of living without him be worse than facing the world's criticism?

What a muttonhead she was. Of course it wouldn't.

She swallowed and stared into Will's beloved face. A face that she'd live with all her life, not struggle to remember as she grew old and bitter.

"Ellen?" Her delay in answering seemed to dent his self-confidence.

"I'll come with ye, Will."

Jubilation blazed in his eyes, turned them gold. "My love..."

"Will, we have to go." She raised a hand to stop him reaching for her. "There's nae time for kisses."

Purpose lit his expression, but to her surprise, instead of pushing the boat into the water, he turned to run back toward the tower.

"Will?" she called out in dismay and confusion. What on earth was he up to?

"I'll only be a minute. Wait there and dinnae move." He stopped then and faced her. "Actually do move. Start bailing."

She growled again, in the grip of too much emotion to make sense of what happened. He loved her. She was mighty grateful about that. But if this delay meant that her father's men caught them, she'd be livid with him forever.

She was bailing like a mad thing and trying to come to terms with the way her life had changed in mere days when Will came bounding down to the beach again. It took her a few seconds to understand what he held in his arms. Once she did, her heart turned over in her breast. The tears that she'd only just conquered welled up again.

"They're my notebooks," she said in wonder, as he shoved the pile of leather-bound volumes at her.

She dropped the bailer and caught them before they could tumble into the water.

He began to push the boat down the sloping beach. "Of course. We cannae leave those behind."

And Ellen, despite the danger, found herself laughing. "You fool. I love ye."

He glanced up with a dazzling smile, as he waded through the waves. "Damn it, you'd better. There's a storage locker in the prow. If you put them in there, they'll stay safe and dry, whatever the weather."

With a vigorous leap, he joined her in the boat and set to rowing away from Bortha.

CHAPTER SEVENTEEN

They were nearly out of the bay when Will heard shouting from the top of the hill behind them. Ellen, who was flinging water out of the boat with the determined concentration that she leveled at most things, lifted her head. "They've arrived."

"And they've discovered you're missing, by the sound of it."

"It's a good thing ye came up with a convincing argument to get me off the island, or we'd still be on the beach."

He and Ellen had only just got away in time, thank God. She must be thinking the same thing, because she cast him a bright-eyed glance as she went back to bailing. In the choppy seas, the little boat bobbed up and down, but he was impressed with how well she kept her balance.

Will redoubled his efforts on the rowing, feeling the pull across his shoulders. As luck had it, the tide was running out, so the current lent him some help. "I'll have to remember that telling you I love ye can win me any fight."

She stopped with the bailer hanging slack from her hand and sent him an adoring look that made him want to kiss her. He reminded himself that right now kissing wasn't a priority. Getting his darling out of her father's clutches was.

"Ye can certainly try that. Often."

He gave a short laugh. Which was all the breath that rowing allowed. "It's a promise. Now keep bailing."

"Aye-aye, captain."

"Now, that's what a man likes to hear."

He'd always loved the sauce in her. He remembered back to his idiot cousin's infatuation with the legend of Fair Ellen. The woman Dougal had described had been a beautiful nonentity, frail and wispy and passive. Will was so glad that the real Ellen turned out to be a complicated creature of fire and determination and cleverness.

His parents would love her. His mother was another woman who paid no heed to received opinions about masculine superiority.

"Dinnae get used to it."

No, he'd better not. Unthinking obedience wasn't Ellen's style. Which would make for an interesting life. Will couldn't wait. He could hardly believe that she'd consented to come with him. Right up to the last minute, he hadn't been sure that she would, although he'd been sure she loved him. The connection between them had always been too profound to pass for mere attraction.

Ellen bent to scoop up more water. Over her shoulder, he watched half a dozen men scrambling down to the beach.

She was doing a braw job of emptying out the bilge. The elegant little boat became more responsive with every minute. Well was this swift craft named for the dolphins that leaped along the channel between Achnasheen and Skye.

A volley of cracks revealed that the guards were armed. Of course they were. They protected a great treasure.

As she looked back, Ellen's face went pale. "Will, they're shooting at us."

"We're out of range. Dinnae fash yourself," he said, even as he put extra heft into his rowing. A flintlock was accurate up to about a hundred yards. The *Leumadair* was well beyond that now.

"If we'd delayed another few minutes, we mightn't have been." She paused. "I'm no' even sure they're aiming at us."

He took a closer look and realized that she was right. "They willnae want to take the chance of hitting the laird's daughter."

More gunshots and shouting, although the men must be as aware as Will was that they wasted their ammunition. The *Leumadair* came up past the point and the last of the skerries sheltering Bortha from this side. He'd soon be able to put up the sail.

"They'll come after us."

"A Mackinnon of Achnasheen cannae be outsailed."

To his surprise, she sent him a mocking grin. "Always so arrogant."

"Aye. But it's true, all the same."

Ellen responded with a snort before she went back to bailing. Her boots must be soaked through. He wished that he'd thought to pick up some shoes for her when he'd gone back to the tower.

"They'll need time to relaunch the boat, then they have to get around the island," she said. "It's surrounded with reefs, so that should hold them up even longer."

"We'll be well away by then."

She looked up. "Well away to where? Are we going to Achnasheen?"

He'd put some thought into this. "No' straightaway. It's too far. My cousin and his wife are on Askaval to the south. That makes more sense as our destination. You're no' dressed for a long journey."

Dougal Drummond and his sparkling, unconventional wife Kirsty lived an unpretentious life on a beautiful island, south of Islay. Will had a suspicion that Ellen would find their company much less daunting than arriving at Achnasheen which was packed with his family. Not to mention that his home was a castle.

He might have done his best to talk his beloved out of her fears of facing curious strangers, but that didn't mean that he lacked sympathy for her. Especially as through force of circumstance, she viewed her lameness and people's reaction to it through her father's eyes.

Will was convinced that she wouldn't find life off Bortha as inhospitable as she dreaded, but he also hoped to ease her into her new world.

Ellen frowned, even as she kept bailing. "Is this the cousin who set out to find me?"

"Aye, that's Dougal." Will watched the men on the island, tiny now in the distance, scatter back over the crest. "You've never met a more dedicated romantic. I swear in his heart, he's still living in the age of chivalry. Now he's someone who really did tumble headlong into believing that soppy myth of Fair Ellen pining away in her tower."

"He never found me."

"No, fate took a hand and delivered him to Kirsty's isle instead. Kirsty is a much more practical creature than he is. You'll like her. She doesnae put up with any nonsense."

Ellen stared at him, neglecting her bailing, although now only an inch or so of water sloshed around in the keel. “Ye sound very fond of them.”

He shrugged and finally stowed the oars. The muscles in his arms and back were on fire. Already he could feel the breeze tousling his hair. Once the sail was up, Brendan MacNeill’s graceful boat would fly like a falcon on the wind. No tub from Bortha had a chance of catching her.

“Of course I’m fond of them, even if as a lad, I wanted to pound some good common sense into Dougal’s head. Since he wed Kirsty, he’s much more down-to-earth.”

“He’s given up all thoughts of Fair Ellen?”

“Aye. Which can only benefit cousinly relations.”

She didn’t laugh at his wry remark. “I dinnae want to cause trouble.”

“Och, we’re a close-knit bunch. I love all my family. I think ye will, too.”

“I hope so.”

The doubt in her voice made his heart crack. “You’ve been unlucky with your kinfolk, *mo chridhe*. I’m offering ye a much nicer selection.”

“And they willnae mind that I’m lame?”

The crack in his heart widened. Her swine of a father had done so much damage. Will wasn’t a fool. He knew years of harm took years of healing, but he swore then and there that before he was done, he’d mend every rip in Ellen’s soul.

“If they do, they’re no’ invited to our Christmas ceilidh.”

She smiled without conviction as he stood and fetched the sail from where it was stowed. With luck and a good wind, they’d be on Askaval by tonight.

Ellen's apprehension mounted as Will's boat glided into the small harbor at what he told her was Askaval. Around them, the summer night descended on the sea. Escaping Bortha had proven easier than she'd expected. Will's claim to be a skillful sailor turned out to be more than idle boasting.

The wind had set fair for the south, and the little boat had raced across the water. They'd gone so fast that she hadn't even seen her father's men in pursuit. She couldn't help feeling that if freedom always felt like this, it would be sweet indeed.

It was a pleasure to watch Will move about the *Leumadair*. Before this, she hadn't realized how he was at home on the water, but the wind and the waves turned out to be his element. She had so much more to discover about the man to whom she'd entrusted her future.

"Dinnae be afraid," he murmured, tightening his embrace. "The Drummonds will be pleased to see us."

She'd spent most of the trip curled up beside Will, while he steered the boat from the seat at the stern. Thank goodness the day was warm so she could take off her waterlogged half boots. They now sat in front of her in the sunlight, but she had an awful feeling that they were ruined forever.

She'd spent a lot of the voyage thinking about Will's family and how they'd react to him showing up with a penniless ragamuffin of a girl at his side. A penniless ragamuffin of a girl with one leg shorter than the other. Now she couldn't help wondering how it felt to anticipate a warm welcome whenever and however one arrived.

Unconditional love had never been part of her life. Although she began to hope that the warmth she saw in Will's eyes when they rested on her might turn out to be just that. "They'll be pleased to see ye."

Will chuckled. "Och, more than that. Dougal will be beside himself to find out that he was right and I was wrong, and that Fair Ellen of the Isles does in fact exist. No' only that, but she's as bonny as rumor paints her. I'm ashamed to admit that I called him a pudding-brained nincompoop when he set out to rescue ye."

"Then ye ended up rescuing me."

He tipped her face up for a quick kiss. "I did indeed, sweetheart."

Ellen blushed. She'd always had a difficult relationship with that stupid nickname, but how could she resent it, when the man she loved told her that she was beautiful? Especially when she knew that Will never lied. "You'll turn my head with all this flattery, my fine laddie."

"And such a pretty head to turn." Finding his balance with enviable swiftness, he stood to haul down the sail and tie the boat up near some stone steps.

"You dinnae seem worried that my father might pursue us."

He shrugged. "Your father has nae idea who stole you away or where to look for ye. If he does happen to track us down, you're of age and out of his legal control. No' to mention that you're now under the protection of the Mackinnon clan. Let him come. If he tries to snatch ye back, he'll find himself facing an army."

Ellen stared at Will in surprise, even as his certainty bolstered her courage. "You're no' afraid?"

"Och, I'll allow nae power on earth to take ye away from me, *mo chridhe*. You're safe from your father. Never doubt it." While she struggled to come to terms with his ardent declaration, he stepped onto the stone quay and held out his hand. "Come, my lady."

Balancing with less grace, she rose. Although she hoped she hid her nerves, she was almost certain that she didn't. Nonetheless she raised her chin. She'd chosen to leave her prison behind and go forth with this man. She refused to start her new life cowering away like a mouse.

"Do ye ken this is the first place I've set foot on other than Bortha in ten years?"

"I do." His smile didn't falter. "The first of many. I'm hoping to take ye to Edinburgh and London and Rome and Paris and Vienna. You've got a whole world to discover, my love. What a privilege for me that you'll discover these places at my side."

"Ye promise me an adventure," she said with a tinge of wistfulness, curling her fingers around his and making a better job of getting out of the boat than she'd feared. Although it was a relief to feel good solid granite under her feet.

Her bare feet.

"Aye, and that's what it will be."

"I'll need some shoes if we're going too far."

"I'll buy ye a thousand pairs of shoes."

"Right now, one pair would be enough."

"You cannae put those boots on. They're no' fit for anything but a fish." Gentle mockery warmed his laugh. "Ye ken, I rather like the idea of carrying away a barefoot bride."

He made everything sound so easy. So much fun.

For so long, she'd felt that life had bound her in chains. Every minute with Will loosened those chains. She sucked in a huge breath of fresh, salt-tinged air and turned to him with a smile. "Then kiss me, Will, and let's see whether your cousin will feed us."

It was hours since they'd finished the food that she'd packed on Bortha. He, like she, must be starving.

"With pleasure." Will drew her into his arms and kissed her until her knees threatened to buckle beneath her.

He raised his head to stare down at her. In the fading light, she read love in his eyes. A love that she realized with a shock had been there almost from the first. Perhaps the unknown Dougal Drummond wasn't the only hopeless romantic in Will's family.

"I think I could live on your kisses alone, my bonny." His hands spanned her waist, while hers draped across his shoulders.

It was her turn for a mocking laugh. "Right now, delightful as your kisses are, I could definitely use a bannock or a morsel of cheese."

"Och, I'm sure we can do better than that. I promised to look after ye, and so far I'm doing a gey poor job of it."

She smiled at him, enchanted anew. "I wouldnae say that."

He gave her another quick kiss. "Let's go and raid my cousin's larder."

By the time Will knocked on the front door of the big gray stone house, he was carrying Ellen. Her bare feet had proven no match for the stones on the road from the quay.

"You cannae spend your life hauling me around," she said, as they waited for the door to open.

"Whisht, lassie. Anyone who knows ye knows you have no trouble standing on your own two feet."

"But your cousins dinnae know me."

"Did ye want to meet them with your feet cut to ribbons?"

No, she didn't. But nor did she want to meet them, windswept from a day on the sea and wearing a simple blouse and kirtle like the poorest crofter on her father's domain. She had enough vanity to wish to make a good impression on the first members of Will's family she encountered.

"Ye can put me down now." She tugged at his hair to make her point.

A point made too late. The door opened to reveal a redheaded giant, who bore enough resemblance to Will for her to guess that he must be Dougal.

Ellen was surprised to see the master of the house answering the door. In general, the upper classes paid servants to greet callers.

The man's handsome face brightened, as the lamps from inside the house revealed who waited on the step. "Good God, it's ye, Will. When you didnae appear on Monday, we feared ye might have drowned." It was said with a notable lack of drama, although Ellen heard affection beneath the unsentimental welcome.

Will's grunt of laughter was dismissive. "No' me, cuz. I'm the best swimmer in the family. Other business occupied my time."

When Dougal's eyes leveled on Ellen, his smile broadened. "Aye, very pretty business, too, I see. Welcome to *Tigh Na Mara*, my lady."

Heat flooded Ellen's cheeks. She felt awkward, too aware of the ragtag impression she must make. "Thank you."

"Dougal, this is Ellen Cameron."

With commendable grace, Dougal bowed and stepped back to allow Will to shoulder his way into the elegant hall. "Your servant, Miss Cameron."

Will went on. "I'm hoping ye can offer us a bath and a change of clothes and a good dinner. And a bed."

"Two beds," Ellen interjected.

Now that she was back in civilization, she was painfully aware of the impropriety of turning up unchaperoned on a stranger's doorstep and in the company of a virile young man. Only a fool would fail to draw the obvious conclusion. Despite Will's description of his cousin as a bit of a dreamer, she could already tell that Dougal Drummond was no fool.

"Two beds," Will said, to her relief.

On Bortha, she'd known that she and Will broke society's rules. But society had felt a thousand miles away. Here, in this lovely house, she was only too conscious that people would assume she was Will's doxy.

"For heaven's sake, Will, the house is ratty with empty bedrooms. Ye can have half a dozen, if you like."

"Dougal, who is it?" A pretty, dark-haired woman in a stylish lemon-yellow dress appeared at the top of the steps. In her arms, she clasped a baby wrapped in a white woolen shawl.

"Good evening, Kirsty." Will's flashing grin reminded Ellen of his devilish side. "We come seeking your hospitality."

Dougal looked up with the kind of smile that Will gave Ellen. "My love, my cousin has turned up, late as usual, and he has company. Come down and meet Miss Ellen Cameron of..."

"Bortha," Will said, as Ellen said, "Inchgallen."

"Och, that's grand." The advent of a pair of salt-encrusted guests so late in the day left Kirsty remarkably unfazed. She made her way down to the hall. "We were expecting a dull evening."

"Thank ye very much," Dougal said with a theatrical humph.

Kirsty wasn't impressed with his response, Ellen could see. "Ye cannae say a bit of company won't go astray, and I can see these two have quite a tale to tell."

"Ye must wonder..." Ellen began.

Kirsty passed the baby to Dougal, who took the child with practiced ease. "Och, save your story for dinner. We cannae do justice to the telling, standing in the hall. You both look altogether done in. Let's get ye organized, then we can have a good blether over a nice plate of roast lamb."

"But do you no' want to know who I am and what I'm doing here?" Ellen asked, taken aback at such unquestioning acceptance. Will had told her that the Drummonds would welcome her. It turned out that he wasn't exaggerating.

Dougal shrugged. "We dinnae stand on ceremony here on Askaval. You're very welcome to our house, Miss Cameron. I hope you'll enjoy your stay."

"Dougal, will ye please tell Ruth that there are another two for dinner and ask the maids to prepare baths? I'll show Miss Cameron to her room. The Chinese one, I think. Will, are ye happy to go into the blue room? It's the one ye usually use here."

"Thank you, Kirsty. That would be braw."

"Ye can put me down now, Will," Ellen muttered, feeling more uncomfortable by the minute.

"Must I?"

"Aye, you must," Kirsty said with a laugh. "I promise to look after the lady and deliver her unharmed to the dining room."

With a sheepish expression, Will let Ellen down to the floor. "She's safe here, I know."

Dougal snickered. "Aye. Whatever ye two have been up to, there's no danger on Askaval. Nae need for you to act like a sheepdog with a ewe lamb, cuz."

"Is it so obvious?" Will asked, then laughed when Kirsty rolled her eyes.

"Aye, it is. Now come and meet Sorcha, the newest member of the family."

Ellen wondered if she was alone in reading Will's reluctance to step away from her. She doubted it. It was obvious that the cousins were very close.

"Hold her." Dougal passed the sleeping baby across. "I've got duties to fulfill."

Ellen was surprised to find Will just as adept with infants as his cousin. Then she remembered that he came from a large family.

Seeing the tiny baby cradled in his strong hands, she couldn't help picturing him holding his own child in the future. Longing twisted deep inside her. This unassuming house and the palpable love between Dougal and Kirsty made her thirst for a life with the same joys. For years, she'd been convinced that normal human pleasures were out of reach. Now she staggered under the possibility that she might become a wife and mother.

"I'm very pleased to meet ye, wee Sorcha," Will murmured in a low croon that made the hairs on Ellen's skin prickle. "What a bonny bairn ye are."

Kirsty watched with a proud maternal smile. "She's quieter than Alexander, at least. We manage as much as three hours sleep a night. I feel positively sprightly, compared to last time."

As Will chuckled, Dougal glanced at Ellen. "Our son and heir was a handful from the start. He's just turned two, and he's still giving us a good run."

Will looked up, eyes soft. "What rubbish. My godson is perfect."

Kirsty's snort expressed her contempt for that remark. "That opinion will no' last, once you've spent twenty-four hours in this house. It's lucky that I love the little terror with all my heart, or I swear we'd run mad. I'm no' sure we haven't."

Dougal turned to Will. "Seeing you're godfather to one perfect child, would ye accept the job for this one, too?"

Will's expression revealed how the request moved him. "I'd be honored."

With a discomfiting mixture of envy and admiration, Ellen observed this domestic harmony. On Bortha, she'd seen Will as a roguish loner who invaded her life and stole her heart away. Now she realized that he was enmeshed in a family and a life that she had no part in. Would he decide that the woman he'd found so enchanting on her rocky island lost her allure, now that he was back in a familiar setting?

If he did, where on earth did that leave her?

When she'd decided to run away with him, she thought she knew him to the soul. But observing him with people he loved and a baby in his arms, she wasn't so sure.

He glanced up and gave her a smile, as if he guessed both her shyness and her misgivings. "Come and see, Ellen."

She took a couple of steps forward, then stopped, self-conscious about her uneven gait. Plague take her, she felt like the monster at the feast. At this moment, all she wanted was to run away and hide from judgmental eyes.

But where could she run? The bitter question reminded her that she couldn't run at all.

Her recklessness in entrusting herself to Will Mackinnon after a mere few days together struck with painful force. She felt a sudden longing for her tower on Bortha, where she knew just where she stood, even if that was on legs of two different lengths.

Will frowned as he studied her face, although she did her best to hide the doubts devouring her. "Ellen?"

She struggled to smile. His expression told her that her efforts failed to convince. He saved her from taking another limping step. He came closer and passed Sorcha across before Ellen had a chance to tell him that she had little experience with babies.

"I'm not..." she began as her arms automatically formed a cradle.

Will supported the little girl's head until Ellen held her the correct way. "Isn't she a wee beauty?"

Tears filled Ellen's eyes, when she stared down at Sorcha. As Will's boat cut through the waves, she'd felt so free. She'd felt as if, with him at her side, she could conquer anything. Now she felt more inadequate than ever. Her father had told her that she wasn't fit to go out into the world. Perhaps he was right.

But the little girl was so warm and soft in her embrace. After a few seconds, Ellen's vision cleared. Wide blue eyes fastened on her face with innocent interest, and the rosebud mouth curved upward in a slow greeting.

Wonder gripped Ellen. "She's smiling at me."

Will stood beside her and despite her fears, she took comfort in his nearness. "Of course she is."

"You're lovely, wee Sorcha," she whispered, touching the baby's cheek with a gentle finger and marveling at the petal-soft skin. "Oh, Will..."

Overwhelmed, she raised her eyes to his. They shared a long look that reminded her that she'd placed her trust in this man and he'd never let her down. Trepidation leached away, and her smile this time was genuine. He flung an arm around her shoulders and hugged her against his side.

When Sorcha grizzled and shifted in Ellen's arms, Kirsty laughed. "She's getting hungry. Let me show ye to your room, Miss Cameron, before she tells us about it."

Ellen's attack of nerves had mostly settled, but she couldn't help seeking signs of disapproval in Kirsty and Dougal's faces. They must have noticed how clumsy she was.

She caught curiosity but no disdain. Given their cousin was hugging a stranger, it was likely that they were curious about more than Ellen's infirmity.

Sorcha grumbled again, and Kirsty took her. "If we'd passed Alexander around at this age, he'd have screamed to the rafters."

Will rolled his eyes. "Aye, I remember. The christening shouldn't be so noisy this time round."

Dougal looked at his cousin. "I'm gey glad you didnae drown, Will. The ceremony wouldn't be the same without ye."

Will moved away from Ellen, as if he understood that her collywobbles had receded. "By God, dinnae smother me in sentimental effusions, laddie. Otherwise I'll start sniveling all over your front hall."

They all laughed, even Ellen, as Kirsty gestured toward the staircase. "Come with me, Miss Cameron. We'll get ye settled."

To her relief, Will took her arm and escorted her upstairs ahead of her hostess.

CHAPTER EIGHTEEN

Ellen was feeling much more capable of confronting her future by the time she'd bathed and dressed. She wore one of Kirsty's gowns, a green silk that rivaled the extravagant wardrobe that her father had given her. To her relief, Kirsty had also lent her some black satin slippers that were only a little too big.

A maid had helped with her toilette, washing the salt from her thick hair and brushing it dry in front of the fire. When Ellen checked the mirror, she was relieved to see an elegant young lady, not a raggle-taggle beggar who looked like she'd been wandering across a stormy heath.

"There, miss. By heaven, you're a bonny lassie." Betsy slid a last pin into the flattering mass of curls she'd piled high on Ellen's head. The girl had a touch with hairdressing that Susie, Ellen's maid on Bortha, had lacked.

Not that the tower contained anyone likely to appreciate a becoming coiffure. Whereas tonight, Ellen was only too aware of the need to impress Will's cousins.

She stared into her face, seeing fear, but also the stirrings of hope. She also saw how she'd changed from the pale, withdrawn creature she'd been before Will's arrival. Her blue eyes contained a knowledge of love that was lacking a week ago.

"Thank you, Betsy." Ellen liked the girl, who hadn't reacted at all to her ungainly descent into the bath. Perhaps Will was right, and the contempt that her limp had sparked in her father's house wasn't the universal reaction.

There was a soft knock on the door.

"Come in," Ellen said, expecting Kirsty or perhaps another of the maids.

Will strode into the room, turning Betsy all goggle-eyed with shock.

"Mr. Mackinnon," she said, curtsying and blushing, although whether at the arrival of a man in an unmarried lady's bedroom or at the magnificent sight he made, Ellen couldn't say.

Ellen had only ever seen Will dressed for the outdoors. Or not dressed at all. In a formal black velvet jacket with silver buttons and a kilt in green and gold, colors she assumed were the Drummond tartan, he took her breath away. His long hair was tied back in a queue, and the snowy-white jabot under his chin emphasized his chiseled jaw.

"I require a few moments of privacy, Ellen," he said. "If that's agreeable to ye."

"Of course." She turned to the maid. "Ye may go, Betsy. Mr. Mackinnon will show me to the dining room."

The girl cast a curious glance between Ellen and Will, before she curtsied again and left. Ellen was sure that her unannounced arrival on Askaval was already subject to speculation belowstairs. If Betsy spread tales of Will invading Ellen's bedroom, the gossip would be unstoppable.

Once they were alone, Ellen rose and stepped toward Will. The first unself-conscious movement that she'd made in this house. "You'll scandalize the household."

His laugh held that warm note that she began to think he kept just for her. "My reputation will never recover. Now, come and kiss me."

How could she resist? Propriety could go to the devil.

Because of his humor, she didn't expect the passion that exploded between them. By the time they drew apart, they were gasping and Ellen was dizzy with pleasure. Then she realized what they'd just done and where she was.

"Will, if my hair is a mess, I'll never forgive ye. Betsy worked on it for hours." A slight overstatement, but it made her point.

He passed a critical eye over her. "No, it looks perfect. In fact ye look perfect."

"Thank you. It's all thanks to Kirsty." Kirsty hadn't just been thoughtful enough to send a selection of dresses, but petticoats and stays and a sheer linen shift with pretty blue cornflowers embroidered across it. And perhaps most welcome of all, she'd sent up a tray of tea and savory pastries and cake. Ellen had fallen on the food with a gusto that would have appalled the waif of her legend. "The way I looked when I arrived, she must have wondered just who you'd brought to her house."

"Och, Kirsty is a tolerant soul. And clever besides. I suspect she's already worked out most of the story."

Will's arms encircled her in a loose embrace. Leaning back against his forearm, she studied that striking face. She noted the marks of weariness – neither of them had slept much over the last few nights, and he'd had a hard day's sailing since – but also the determination. Even despising the myth of Fair Ellen of the Isles, she couldn't help feeling that it reached a suitable conclusion.

In the end, a hero had rescued her.

"You know you shouldnae be in here," she said, wishing she sounded like she meant it.

"I'm starting to miss the tower." He heaved an exaggerated sigh. "There I only had to worry about ye shooting me."

"And my father's guards."

"Och, they didn't frighten me half as much as ye did. Kiss me again, Ellen. It feels like a century since I last held you in my arms."

"Oh, Will," she whispered, helpless against her love for him.

This time, the kiss sent her floating up toward heaven. When she came back to earth, he was sitting in an armchair by the fire and she lay in melting surrender across his lap.

When she surveyed him with dazed eyes, she couldn't help giggling. And giggling was something foreign to her former solemn self. "I'll have to call Betsy back."

He inspected her with bright hazel eyes. "You're looking a little ruffled, but quite acceptable."

"You're no'." She reached out and combed her fingers through the rich auburn hair falling about his face. "You look like a Highlander of old."

By the time the next bout of kissing came to a halt, she too cursed their lack of privacy. "I'm so glad ye stopped by, but it's been an awfu' long time since breakfast." Despite the refreshments, Ellen was famished. "Shall we go downstairs?"

His expression turned serious. "I didnae just call in to kiss you, Ellen."

Puzzled, she stared at him. "What is it?"

His voice lowered to a rumble, as it always did when his strongest feelings were engaged. "I think I should stand up to say this."

She scrambled off his knees and stared down at him. "Will, you're making me nervous."

"I need to talk to ye before we meet Kirsty and Dougal again." He rose more slowly than she had. "That's why I invaded your bedroom and let propriety go hang."

He still sounded uncharacteristically stern. But Ellen reminded herself that she'd gambled so much on trusting him. She had to keep trusting him.

Leveling her shoulders, she met his eyes. They glowed with familiar radiance. That was reassuring. "Propriety has had little to do with what we've done together."

To her relief, faint amusement entered his gaze. "For which I'm very grateful. If I'd met ye in the ordinary course of things, we'd have managed a few polite chats over tea or perhaps a walk in the rose garden. All under a chaperone's beady eye."

She noticed that he didn't mention dancing, but put the thought away before it could smart. "If you'd wanted to court me."

The amusement deepened, placing attractive creases around his eyes. "Och, I'd have courted ye, lassie. Never doubt it."

"I'd have liked that."

"Aye. We havenae done anything in the normal way, which is why I'm trying to do this part right." He ran a hand through his curtain of hair. "And making a fair dog's dinner of it, too."

She stared at him wide-eyed. As she held out her hands, expectation and hope tangled together in her stomach. An incoherent prayer formed that she didn't mistake what this meant.

When he took her hands in a firm grip, her heart crashed against her ribs. "What...what are ye trying to do, Will?"

Her heart gave another of those disconcerting lurches, as he dropped to his knees before her. His gaze didn't shift from hers. He looked intent and grave. And a little unsure of himself, which buttressed her confidence. As a rule, Will Mackinnon wasn't subject to self-doubt. Most of the time, she approved of his assured attitude to even the thorniest issue, such as whether her father's guards were likely to shoot them. But right now, she liked that he didn't seem too sure about what she might say.

"Ellen... Miss Cameron..."

She refrained from pointing out that she hadn't been Miss Cameron to him since their earliest interactions. His grip on her hands tightened, as if he feared that she might run away. Silly man, didn't he know that she was just where she wanted to be?

Will swallowed, and she saw his Adam's apple bob. More appealing uncertainty. She liked that he didn't take her answer to his proposal for granted. This had to be the overture to a proposal. Not even someone as unworldly as she was could be wrong about that.

"Ellen, I want ye to feel no obligations toward me. I ken we havenae been together long and that you fear you have no real choice in what happens next. But I swear on every one of my gallant Mackinnon ancestors that if you'd rather make your own way, I'll see you have the means to do whatever you wish. Ye might prefer to pursue your writing and research in Edinburgh. Or London even. Ye might want to travel. I didnae help you to escape from Bortha just so you became a prisoner once again."

She bit back a protest. Because she realized that he was only answering the objections she'd made on Bortha. Back when she'd let fear convince her that she was better off in her lonely tower than committing herself to this splendid man.

"That's...that's very good of ye, Will," she said, wondering why he imagined that she remained that frightened creature. He'd accused her of being a prisoner in her mind as much as physically. He'd been right. But when she set sail at Will's side, she'd cast aside her shackles.

He shook his head. "It's no'. It's only fair."

For a fleeting instant when she came to Askaval, she'd wondered what would happen to her if Will decided that he didn't want her. Now she paused and took time to consider what he offered. So many of the things that she'd never dared to dream about when she was confined on Bortha. Independence. A chance to find her own way. A life dedicated to scholarship.

Once, before she'd met Will, they might have tempted her. No longer. Instead everything sounded like more loneliness. And if she married him, she was sure that she could do most of those things anyway.

When he'd fallen to his knees, she'd prepared for declarations and promises. She supposed that what Will had said counted as both. He gave her a choice, because he knew that choice had been a rare luxury.

"I...revere your generosity," she said slowly. "But what you're saying doesnae require you to kneel before me."

Will didn't smile. He was on edge, although after what they'd done and said, he must guess that she'd like nothing better than to become his wife.

"The other offer I mean to make does."

Ellen had to fight not to smile and kiss him and say yes, yes, yes. After all, he hadn't yet asked the important question. Her voice was steady. "Then perhaps ye should make it."

"Ellen, I love ye. I want to spend my life with ye." At last he smiled, turning her wayward heart to sugar. "Will you do me the great honor of marrying me?"

"Will…"

He went on before she could finish her answer. "I promise that nae woman in Scotland will be more cherished. I promise that ye have my heart now and forever. I promise that come what may, my first loyalty will always be to you."

Will stared up into her face, eyes golden and glowing. She swallowed to moisten a dry mouth, and her fingers tangled in his as if she never meant to let him go.

She didn't. He was hers. She was his. On Bortha when he'd proclaimed her as his destiny, he was right. From the moment that he'd climbed up her tower, her fate was sealed.

Ellen didn't note the lengthy silence, until the light in his eyes dimmed. "My darling? What do ye think?"

She realized that she stared at him, dumbstruck with joy. Which meant that she hadn't yet answered him. Although she couldn't think why he'd doubt her response.

A great lump of emotion blocked her throat. It took her a few seconds to clear it.

Because she was happy and because Will had taught her that laughter could enrich any moment, she dared to tease him a little. "I was wondering if ye had any more of those wonderful things to say."

"I'm sure I could find some." He paused and narrowed his eyes at her. "Do I need to?"

Ellen gave a choked laugh. "No. But it was nice to hear them."

"No, because the answer is no?" From his face, she saw that he already knew what her response was. She wasn't alone in liking to tease.

"This isnae the first time you've said that you want to marry me."

"Aye, I knew what I wanted almost from the beginning. But I dinnae think I ever got around to phrasing the idea as a question."

She gave a low chuckle. "No, as I recall, you were a wee bit more autocratic than that. It's lovely to hear the words and have a chance to express my approval for your plans."

"And ye do approve?"

She lifted their joined hands and kissed his knuckles with all the love crammed into her heart. When she raised her head, the impulse to amusement had evaporated. Instead her soul overflowed with love and thankfulness.

"The answer is yes. How could it be anything else? I love ye, Will. That will never change. Take me home to Achnasheen, and let's be blissfully happy for the rest of our lives. I cannae wait."

His expression flared into burning exultation. If ever she'd questioned his love, she never would again. His clumsiness as he stumbled to his feet betrayed his overwhelming emotion.

"My forever love," he sighed, as he swept her into his arms for a dizzying kiss.

CHAPTER NINETEEN

Will and Ellen were very late heading downstairs. When a man received a loving commitment from the woman he adored, one kiss wasn't nearly enough to seal the deal. Only when Ellen reminded him, with a reluctance he rejoiced to hear, that they owed a duty to their hosts, did he recall that this wasn't his house and that bedding his beloved right now would shame her.

Even that reminder of society's rules couldn't stop him from kissing her again and again.

"Why are ye smiling?" Ellen asked, as they paused outside the drawing room door.

"Because I'm happy." He glanced across at her. "And because I hope we dinnae run into Betsy. She'll want my guts for garters."

Ellen raised a nervous hand to her hair, now more an untidy tumble than a coiffure. His eyes caught on the heavy signet ring that gleamed on her left hand. Somewhere amongst all the kissing, he'd found time to slide his ring onto her finger.

"Do ye think the Drummonds will notice?"

"No."

"Fibber," she said affectionately, hooking her fingers around his crooked elbow.

In truth, given what he knew about his cousins' marriage, Will would wager half his inheritance that the physical attraction raging between Will and Ellen was no news to them. "You speak such sweet endearments to me, beloved. I'm quite overcome."

She snorted, as he pushed the door open to catch Kirsty and Dougal kissing in front of the unlit hearth.

"Will... Miss Cameron..." a flushed Kirsty stammered, although she didn't move far from her big, brawny husband. "Ye were so long coming downstairs that we..."

"Decided to take up your favorite pastime?" Will asked in a dry tone.

"A laddie needs something to keep his mind off his empty stomach," Dougal retorted.

"I had to talk to Ellen."

"It must have been a braw long discussion." With a knowing tilt of one russet eyebrow, Dougal surveyed the two of them. Will was more certain than ever that his cousin had guessed that he was head over heels in love with the beautiful girl who held his arm.

He didn't mind. He and Dougal were the same age, and his cousin was as much a brother to him as any of his actual brothers.

"It was." Will drew Ellen further into the room. A quick glance at her face told him that she looked proud and happy. He'd noticed that her limp worsened when she thought people were staring at her. But tonight she moved more smoothly than usual. A heaviness in her eyes hinted that her mind lingered on their passionate kisses upstairs. "I'm delighted to tell ye that Miss Cameron has agreed to become my wife."

He hadn't been sure how the announcement would go down. After all, Ellen was a stranger, although he was sure that Dougal and Kirsty would love her once they got to know her. But if anyone should understand love at first sight, it was his cousin.

Nothing would change Will's mind about Ellen being the woman of his heart, but after years of isolation, she was shy. She was also worried about how his family would greet his betrothal to a woman who was lame. So much depended on this first encounter between Ellen and his kin.

To his relief, Kirsty and Dougal didn't let him down. Dougal gave a pleased laugh and strode across to clap him on the back. "Well done, old son. No' that I'm at all surprised. I could see ye were besotted, the moment you came through the door."

"Thanks, cuz." Will didn't argue. He was besotted. "I'm the luckiest man in the world."

"Ye are indeed." Dougal turned to Ellen. "Let me welcome you into the family, Miss Cameron."

"Thank you," she said, as Dougal bent to kiss her cheek.

Kirsty approached the happy trio. "Will, I'm so glad for ye and Miss Cameron."

When she hugged him, he had to release Ellen, who he saw was taken aback at this exuberant response to their engagement. "Thank you."

"Congratulations." Kirsty turned to Ellen with a beaming smile. "I hope you'll be as happy as Dougal and I are."

"I'm sure we will be," Ellen said, as Kirsty embraced her, too.

Will felt a pleasant surprise to hear her sounding so optimistic. He realized in that moment that Ellen had dedicated herself heart and soul to their future. Warmth flooded him. It was a brave act from a brave woman. What a treasure he'd unearthed on Bortha's forbidding shore.

"Miss Cameron, you'll have to tell us all about how ye and Will met. We had no idea he was contemplating matrimony."

When Will heard Ellen's dry chuckle, he knew that she was fine. She didn't need his help to find her place at *Tigh na Mara*. "I doubt very much if he was."

Will smiled at her, so proud that he was ready to burst. He was well aware that he asked a great deal of her and that after her captivity on Bortha, finding her place in the outside world would be a challenge. Especially when her infirmity had already made her an outcast from her family. But he could already see that the qualities he loved – her intelligence and courage and ardent heart – would earn her a place of honor wherever she went.

Kirsty caught Ellen's hands and stood back to survey her with approval. "I'm glad ye changed his mind for him, Miss Cameron."

"One look at Ellen, and I was ready to call the banns," Will said, earning him a roll of the eyes from his beloved for his trouble.

"Was that while I threatened to shoot ye?" she asked sweetly.

Will saw Kirsty and Dougal observe Ellen with growing respect. "Good for ye, Miss Cameron," Dougal said. "There have been plenty of moments, when for two pins, I'd have shot this rogue, too."

"Tell us more," Kirsty said. "Will always has the lassies begging for his attention. He's the one who needs a gun to fight them off."

"Now, Kirsty, that's an exaggeration," he said in discomfort.

"No, it's no'."

No, it wasn't. But he wasn't sure that he wanted his bride to know what a devil he'd been with the ladies.

"I'm sure it's no'," Ellen said. "He was revoltingly sure that he could charm his way out of trouble." She paused. "The problem is that he can. From the day we met, I was as lost as he was."

Will couldn't resist responding to that confession with a quick kiss that left her rosy-cheeked and flustered. When she struggled out of his arms, Ellen's smile was close to natural.

She turned to Dougal and Kirsty. "I think ye should both call me Ellen, given I'm going to be part of the family."

Dougal looked thoughtful. "I've always had a soft spot for girls called Ellen."

It was Kirsty's turn to roll her eyes. "No' this again." She spoke to Ellen. "When I met this great galoot, he was madly in love with a mythical creature he'd never laid eyes on called Fair Ellen of the Isles. You wouldnae believe the trouble it took me to make him realize that she was a fairy tale and he belonged here with me."

"Och, Kirsty love, ye should be kinder to Fair Ellen. Without her, I'd never have washed up on the shores of Askaval to become your lord and master."

Kirsty snorted at that. As well she might. Dougal and Kirsty's was a marriage of equals, where his romantic imagination lent wings to her more practical nature.

"You know, I wouldnae altogether say she's a myth," Ellen said slowly.

Dougal and Kirsty both regarded her with sudden rapt attention. "Just where did ye two meet?" Kirsty asked.

Will decided to come to Ellen's rescue. "On Bortha."

"I've never heard of it," Dougal said.

"No, it's well to the west and away from the shipping lanes, and there's no' much there. Until the storm blew me off course, I had nae idea it even existed."

He watched as the incredible truth dawned on his hosts. Their astonishment had him hiding a smile. "And I suppose Ellen was living in her father's house and they offered ye shelter?" Dougal asked. That was what had happened to him four years ago, when he met Kirsty.

"In a manner of speaking," Ellen said.

"But she said she tried to shoot him," Kirsty pointed out.

"It was my father's house – even if he doesnae live there," Ellen said. Will could see that she started to enjoy teasing Dougal and Kirsty.

"It wouldnae be a tower with a braw strong lock?" Kirsty asked.

"It's as if ye were there," Will said with mock admiration.

Dougal gave a startled laugh and slung one powerful arm across his wife's slender shoulders. "Are ye saying, cuz, that you won the prize after all? Ye rescued Fair Ellen of the Isles from captivity?"

A smug smile curved Will's lips. "I've always been the most heroic member of the family."

Dougal ignored that. "Yet ye ragged me without mercy about what a pea brain I was to imagine she was real."

Will realized he didn't have too much cause for gloating – apart from the fact that he'd won the bride of his heart. "Aye, well, I might owe ye a small apology for that."

As if he was hard of hearing, Dougal placed one hand up to his ear. "What was that ye said?"

Will laughed. "I said I'm sorry I called ye a cork-witted ass. You were right, and I was wrong."

"Ah, better," Dougal said. He turned to Ellen, who watched the byplay between the cousins with an arrested expression. Will supposed that she wasn't used to seeing a loving family in action. He vowed then and there that they'd create a loving family of their own.

"Ellen, I can hardly believe that my cousin found you and liberated you – and even better fell in love with ye. It's a credit to the family."

Ellen laughed at that. "I'm pleased to be of service."

Dougal's smile softened, and he hugged Kirsty closer. "On a personal level, I owe ye a huge debt. If your legend hadnae spread across the Highlands, I'd never have set out in search of you and I'd never have met my darling Kirsty. And that would have left me a beggar at life's feast."

Kirsty's expression melted, and she drew Dougal down for a kiss. "Thank ye for that."

"Well said," Will murmured.

Kirsty regarded Ellen with a concerned frown. "These laddies carry on as if this was all a grand adventure, but ye must have suffered if you were locked away."

Ellen made a sweeping gesture. "Obviously there's more to the story, but it's going to take time to tell. As you guessed, it's no' an altogether happy tale. Tonight is for celebrations. I'm safe, and Will and I are to wed. Let's leave the sadder parts of my history until another day."

Dougal glanced at the clock. "I have so many questions, but let's talk over dinner. Ruth will be fuming, if we put things back again."

Will raised a hand to gain his cousin's attention. "Before we go in, can I ask ye to talk to the minister here? I'd like to marry Ellen tomorrow."

He wanted to make her his as soon as possible, and there was the added incentive of heading off a scandal. The story of Fair Ellen's rescue would spread across Scotland like wildfire. He wanted to quash any gossip about the maiden and her rescuer anticipating their wedding vows.

"Of course," Dougal said.

"A wedding on Askaval. How exciting." Kirsty's eyes sparkled with excitement. "We havenae had one of those since my father married Ada two years ago."

Will turned to Ellen. "Does that suit ye, *mo chridhe*?"

She looked overwhelmed, but unafraid. He loved that she embraced her future with such spirit. "If Dougal and Kirsty dinnae mind."

Kirsty smiled at Ellen with the warmth so essential to her nature. Will could already see that Ellen had found a friend in his cousin's wife. "We dinnae mind a bit, but why don't we put off the nuptials for a day or two? It would give us a chance to plan a party and make you a dress fit for the occasion. It would also give ye time to rest before the ceremony. Even without knowing the full story, I can see you've had an eventful time. Why no' take a little while to catch your breath before ye become a bride?"

Will read disappointment on Ellen's face, even as he bit back a groan of his own. It seemed that he wasn't the only one seething with lust. He'd been very much looking forward to a wedding night before too long.

On the other hand, so many pleasures had been stolen from Ellen. He could imagine the idea of a real wedding celebration might appeal to her and give her happy memories to cherish. And she was tired after their tumultuous days on Bortha, followed by their voyage today. By God, so was he. A quiet interval before he became a bridegroom wasn't a bad idea at that.

"Ellen, what do ye think?"

She took a moment to consider then nodded her head. "Kirsty and Dougal, you're both so terribly kind, given I've arrived without warning and without any belongings of my own. But, aye, I'd like to look like a bride on my wedding day."

Kirsty smile broadened. "Och, it's the least we can do. Will is like a brother to us, and I'm hoping that means I gain a sister, when ye become his wife."

The wholehearted acceptance left Ellen looking overcome. For ten years, she'd been heartbreakingly alone. Soon she'd become a man's wife, and it seemed that she was acquiring a family as well. Perhaps an opportunity to find her place in this new world before her wedding wasn't too much to ask after all.

"Thank ye." To Will's surprise, Ellen hugged Kirsty. He'd always thought that she'd be reticent with strangers. Perhaps Kirsty's unconditional approval lowered her defenses. "A wedding in a couple of days it shall be."

"Capital." Dougal gazed on with a beaming smile. "I have a feeling it will take ye more than tonight's dinner to tell us everything anyway."

When Ellen shot Will a wry glance that said she had no intention of sharing everything that had happened between them, he burst out laughing.

CHAPTER TWENTY

As it was, the ceremony didn't take place for another week. Will soon realized that his parents would hate to miss their eldest son's nuptials, not to mention that he was eager to show his bride off to his closest family. So the day after Ellen and Will's arrival on Askaval, messages went off to Achnasheen, inviting the laird and his lady to a wedding.

His parents and brothers and sisters, along with various spouses and offspring, had arrived last night, agog with curiosity about Will's mysterious betrothed. As his older sister Grainne put it, Will had spent his life steering clear of the parson's mousetrap. The lady who caught him must be special indeed.

Of that, he had no doubt. He'd fallen in love quickly, but every day brought new and fascinating revelations about the woman he adored. Ellen soon found her place on Askaval, and the welcome Dougal and Kirsty gave her meant that while she was nervous about meeting his mother and father, she wasn't too self-conscious to make a favorable impression.

As the shadows that had crowded around her on Bortha receded, she became lovelier than ever. She'd feared that strangers would treat her as an oddity, but nobody paid her infirmity much attention. By now, Will seldom noticed any unevenness in her walk. It was just a part of her, the way sparkling blue eyes and rich golden hair were part of her.

It was too soon for him to judge how she'd cope with his parents. They'd all spent the evening together, and signs were good that initial goodwill might mature into something more lasting.

Now he stood in a fever of impatience at the altar in Askaval's pretty little church. He couldn't wait to claim Ellen as his bride.

The week had been so busy that he'd had to survive on stolen kisses. Not for the first time, he blessed the storm that had granted him those days alone with her. Right now, carnal hunger was eating him alive. Ever since she'd agreed to marry him, he'd burned. Despite the many shocking things that he and Ellen had done to each other, the final intimacy was yet to come.

He had a stern word with his carnal hunger, because he was in a church and he loved Ellen for much more than just the way that she stirred his masculine instincts. The carnal hunger paid him no heed.

"Stop it," Dougal murmured at his side. He was dressed in a formal black velvet jacket and the Drummond tartan in green and gold. Will was similarly attired, although his kilt was in the Mackinnon colors of red and black.

"Stop what?"

"Thinking about what you'd like to do to Ellen when ye get her alone. It's no' seemly."

"How did you..." Then he shut up. Of course Dougal knew. He'd been a bridegroom four years ago, and his love for his wife included a healthy dose of earthy satisfaction. "You're right. I should be ashamed of myself. But a week's a long time, and we've hardly had a minute alone. It's driving me up the wall."

Dougal's knowing chuckle died when he met the minister's repressive stare. He had the grace to blush and shuffle his feet. "Aye, Ellen and Kirsty have been closeted away on wedding business every day. You're no' the only one feeling neglected, cuz."

Dougal didn't appear to mind too much, Will noted. "The world owes Ellen a proper wedding."

"Aye," Dougal said, and this time he didn't sound like he wanted to laugh. Dougal and Kirsty had been outraged when they learned the details of Ellen's captivity.

Will cast a glance across the packed church. Gus Macbain, Kirsty's father and the Laird of Askaval, had returned from his travels with his wife – and Will's aunt – Ada. Will's parents Callum and Mhairi occupied a front pew, with his brothers and sisters and their spouses and children spread about them. All looked in high spirits, thank heaven. His younger brother Sebastian sent him a wink and a thumbs up of encouragement.

Will wanted to give his beloved the world, but the first thing he wanted to give her was a family. She'd been alone and undervalued too long.

Kirsty was absent, because she acted as Ellen's attendant. Ada held wee Sorcha who was living up to her reputation as a placid baby. Dougal had had stern words with his two-year-old son Alexander about the importance of this day for his adored godfather. So far that lecture seemed to be taking effect, although Will wouldn't wager a groat on the good behavior lasting past the ceremony.

The rest of the congregation included friends from Askaval. Since Dougal's marriage, Will had found a second home on this beautiful island. If he'd ever thought about marriage – and he hadn't very often – back in his bad old days, he'd imagined wedding in the medieval chapel at Achnasheen. Yet today it seemed only right that he and Ellen should make their vows on an island. After all, it was another island that had brought them together. And given that none of her kin attended the ceremony, he liked that they plighted their troth here where the world wasn't all Mackinnon.

A murmur rose outside. The islanders who hadn't been able to find a place in the church were crowded around the doors to see the bride arrive. Will's heart gave a great thud as if to remind him that from this moment, his life changed forever.

"Nervous?" Dougal whispered.

"No' a bit of it," Will replied, and he meant it to his soul. He wasn't a superstitious man, but he believed what he'd said to Ellen back on Bortha. She was born to be his.

The organ in the loft started to play something slow and solemn, and the congregation stood with a rustle.

Kirsty stepped into the church, carrying a bouquet of summer roses from *Tigh na Mara's* gardens. She was wearing a deep blue gown that was dashed becoming. She glanced up to where Will and Dougal waited and gave them a misty smile.

Then everything but the sight of Ellen faded from Will's vision. Illuminated in a ray of sunlight, she paused in the arched stone doorway. She stood straight and proud, and the radiant joy on her face made the bright day seem dull by comparison. She'd pinned her heavy golden hair into an elaborate arrangement with pearls and flowers. More pearls decorated her simple cream silk dress. She, too, held a bouquet of roses, cream to match her gown.

He'd wondered if she'd be a shy bride. She was among strangers, and she was sensitive about her limp. But she swept into the church like a queen claiming her kingdom.

In Ellen's presence, his heart always found itself performing acrobatics. Now it swelled so huge with gratitude that this marvelous woman had agreed to marry him that it threatened to break free of his chest. What a lucky devil he was.

The breath escaped his lungs in a gasp of admiration as she started down the aisle. He never cared about her lameness, except for the way it affected her view of herself. At this moment, Ellen moved as if her uneven gait was no flaw, but just one more aspect of her dazzling beauty.

It took him a second to realize that unlike every other wedding ceremony he'd ever attended, no man accompanied the bride. Instead she approached him, solitary and incandescent with happiness. With a shock, he realized that this was just how it should be. Ellen made a gift of herself to the man she loved.

Will swallowed to shift the jagged boulder of emotion blocking his throat and blinked to clear the moisture from his eyes. If ever he wanted to see everything, it was now.

"By heaven, she's beautiful," Dougal said beside him, and Will heard an echo of his own awe in his cousin's remark. "And brave."

"Aye, she's a remarkable woman," he said in a raw voice. Will had always known it, but as Ellen made her way down the aisle, he thanked God that at last she recognized the truth, too.

He thought that he couldn't be prouder of her until the minister asked, "Who giveth this woman to be married to this man?"

Ellen answered in her clear contralto, "I give myself to William Mackinnon for as long as I shall live."

"My darling, I love ye," he murmured, taking her hand. When she smiled into his eyes, he recognized a love that would sustain him for the rest of his days. With happiness overflowing from his heart, he kept hold of her hand and turned to face the altar.

CHAPTER TWENTY-ONE

Will knocked on the door leading from his dressing room to the bedroom Dougal and Kirsty had given them for their wedding night. It was late. The celebrations had turned into a wild ceilidh with music and dancing that continued past midnight. The islanders of Askaval loved a party. Around him now, an expectant silence ranged, although he knew the house was packed with guests.

Or perhaps the expectant silence was part of the gratitude that he'd felt all day, since this morning when he'd committed his life to Ellen Cameron. The day had been crammed with happiness and excitement, but powerful emotion kept catching him out, as he realized that she was his. He'd won her, and now they set out together to create their future.

A wee touch of triumph was forgivable. After all, he'd feared that Ellen's terror of facing the world might outweigh her love for him. But mostly he was just bloody thankful. He didn't know what he'd done to deserve this glorious woman, but whatever it was, he was forever beholden to fortune for smiling on him.

And of course, there was desire. When he thought of Ellen, there would always be desire.

He'd wanted to whisk her away and have his wicked way as soon as he'd spoken his vows. But aside from what he owed to Dougal and Kirsty for the trouble that they'd taken over the wedding, Ellen had been so overjoyed to find such a welcome with his family and the people of Askaval. She'd even managed to dance, letting Will support her when her balance failed.

He hadn't had the heart to bring the party to an early end. But now at last, God be praised, passion would reign. His blood pounded with masculine intent, and expectation churned in his gut.

This time when he came to her bed, there would be no fear and no danger and no restrictions. He was hard and heavy under his brocade robe – his parents had brought him some of his belongings, including the fine clothes that he'd worn for his wedding, and his late grandmother's wedding ring. He hadn't fancied standing up before the minister in borrowed finery, although he'd have attended the ceremony naked, if it meant he got to call Ellen his bride.

Ellen seemed to take an age to bid him to enter, but he supposed it couldn't really be so long. He was at the mercy of an appetite that turned any delay into a torment.

For the first time in his life, Will trembled at the prospect of possessing a woman. But then no woman had ever meant so much to him. The hand that pushed the door wide was shaking, and the legs that carried him across the threshold were unsteady.

He paused, captivated anew by her unique beauty. "Ellen..."

Candles flickered from every surface in the room, transforming her into a creature of light and shadow. She sat up in a large carved bed, with the sheets pulled to her waist. Her wisp of a pink silk nightdress did little to conceal her full breasts. Luxuriant hair tumbled loose around her bare shoulders, and her eyes glowed with sensual interest, as she subjected him to an equally detailed inspection.

Will was hellish glad that she'd undressed. The way he felt at this moment, he was likely to rip her stylish wedding gown to rags in his eagerness.

She smiled with an unabashed anticipation that made his blood pump even harder. "Ye took forever."

"This week took forever. Now you're all mine."

Her eyes continued to devour him. "And you're all mine."

"Aye, that I am, my darling." He moved across to the sideboard, where the servants had set out a bottle of claret, a couple of glasses, and a tray of food. "Would ye like a glass of wine?"

"No." That ravenous gaze ranged over him in a way that made him crazy with need. "Perhaps later."

His gesture was self-deprecating. "I want ye to know that you've married a civilized man and no' a wild animal."

She gave a low laugh. "I ken that you're a perfect knight, Will. I ken that better than anyone."

Ellen was remembering their nights on Bortha. So was he.

Part of him wanted to argue with that overly kind description. Most of him, however, loved her high opinion of him, however unmerited. He prayed that he never proved her wrong.

"I also hope ye understand that while I want ye like the very devil, I also love and respect you."

Amusement brightened her eyes to sapphire. "Noted."

"So if I leap on ye like a starving man, I'm doing it with more than lascivious impulses."

"Lascivious impulses sound good." Her smile told him that she wanted him almost as much as he wanted her, and her voice held a note of fond impatience. "Will, come over here and kiss me. This last week has lasted an eternity. I've wanted so much to be alone with ye. Dinnae make me wait any longer. You're no' the only one who has hankered and wondered."

Elation rang in his laugh as he strode to the bed, letting his robe fall in a heap on the Turkey carpet.

Will swept Ellen up into a whirlwind. He moved so fast, she didn't even get a chance to appreciate his magnificent nakedness. He kissed her madly, passionately, rapaciously, and she met him every step of the way. This was how he'd kissed her on Bortha. As though even if the world slammed to an end around them, he couldn't stop.

He only lifted his head when he dragged off her nightdress and flung it to the floor. His greedy hands shoved down the covers to reveal her body. When he kneeled over her, he caged her against the sheets.

This was a captivity that she welcomed. Will's love had set her free in all the ways that mattered.

With breathtaking ardor, he touched her in all the secret, magical places that he'd discovered in the big bed in her tower, until she was writhing and gasping under his caresses.

She cradled his head between her hands, forcing him to meet her eyes. For a fleeting instant, her attention strayed to the simple gold ring that marked her as his wife for the rest of her life. "Will, I want ye. I've wanted ye too long. Make me yours."

"It's likely I'll hurt ye." Desperation lit his gaze and his answer was strained. "The first time anyway."

Ellen bumped her hips up until they met his rampant virility. A shudder of bone-deep excitement gripped her, as she rubbed against him in brazen impulse. With a guttural groan, he closed his eyes. His face contracted as if he was in pain, but after Bortha, she knew that desire could hover as close to agony as to pleasure.

"It hurts wanting ye like this," she forced out of a tight throat. "Nothing you do to me can be worse than suffering this need I have for ye."

When he opened his eyes, she caught a flash of the devil-may-care rogue who had first stolen her heart. She'd soon realized that he was so much more than that seductive pirate, but something in her rejoiced to see that her pirate was still there. "Och, it's no' that bad, *mo chridhe*. I'm almost sure you'll survive the experience."

Ellen didn't smile back. She was too close to the edge. "I dinnae damn well care if I don't. Come inside me, Will. Come...home."

His eyes softened. "Och, Ellen, ye break my heart, even as you make me the happiest man in Scotland."

He shifted to lie between her thighs. He'd touched her down there already, caressing her into slickness. The scent of need tinged the air with sensual promise.

She ran her hands up his chest and hooked them over his shoulders. His loose auburn hair created a curtain about her cheeks, as he explored her mouth with an unfettered craving that thrilled her to the marrow.

Instinctively she pressed higher, closing her knees tight against his hips. He tilted forward, then raised his head and stared at her as if his world began and ended with her. She became aware of an unfamiliar pressure between her legs. When she couldn't stifle a faint sound of discomfort, he tautened.

"Will, dinnae stop." She appreciated his care for her – how could she not? But she was frantic to know what it was like when he moved inside her.

"I don't want to hurt ye."

"I want this. I've wanted this since ye first touched me on Bortha." She bowed up to take more of him. "I need to be part of you. I need ye to be part of me."

The connection of their eyes remained unbroken, so she watched her pleading find a place in his heart. His gaze turned dark with poignant emotion, and when he kissed her, she felt that his lips delivered his soul into her keeping.

"I love ye, Ellen."

The words settled deep. Any lingering doubts about her fitness as a mate for this superb male vanished forever. She dug her fingers into his sinewy shoulders and raised her knees. "So show me."

He changed the angle of his body and tightened his hips. Holding her gaze in a silent vow of adoration, he advanced.

Will was right. It did hurt. Ellen bit her lip to muffle a cry of pain, but even so, a whimper escaped. He stopped again.

He stretched her beyond capacity. She remembered holding his erect rod on Bortha. It had seemed large then. Right now, with him inside her, it felt enormous.

"Breathe, my darling," he muttered.

Colored lights flashed in front of her eyes. She realized that she was holding her breath. Some of her pain came from lungs screaming for air. With a choked laugh, she sucked in a gulp of air, then another. Her tension eased, and with that, the worst of her discomfort.

"Better?" he asked.

"Aye, better."

He shifted further. Shaking hands caught her knees and bent them higher. That felt better, too.

All this wasn't nearly as unpleasant as it had been at first. Her body adjusted to his invasion. She might even say some of it was enjoyable. She loved being so close to Will.

Aye, this wasn't too bad at all.

She might almost say...

"Will!" she gasped, when he thrust then withdrew with a leisurely care that sent a great wave of heat gushing through her.

As he pushed inside, he chuckled. This time, pleasure overcame any slight discomfort. At the end of the thrust, he lingered, before drawing back with another sensuous glide. "Ye like this?"

"Oh, yes," she sighed, as he joined their bodies yet again. She clenched around him, reveling in his growl of approval.

So often, she'd imagined what it would be like to give herself to Will. What they'd done already had provided a taste of fulfilment. But nothing they'd done before, however titillating, however delightful, hinted at this unparalleled intimacy. It was as if the physical expression of their love melded them into one being.

He set up a driving rhythm. Every time he slid into her, she felt as though his entire body said, "I love you."

Soon delight transformed into the irresistible rise to bliss that she'd discovered in his arms on Bortha. She surrendered to the rapturous upward spiral and broke free into quaking, panting spasms, even as Will plunged hard and groaned his release. She clasped him to her trembling body as liquid warmth flooded her womb.

"Will, I do love ye," she murmured.

Tears thickened her voice. Tears of surpassing joy. How close she'd come to missing out on this. The thought only made her hold her husband nearer, here in the radiant aftermath of that transcendent journey.

Will lifted his head to stare down at her with a light in his eyes that she'd never seen before. "After tonight, you're no longer Fair Ellen of the Isles, but Fair Ellen, my dearest beloved."

How she'd changed. How he'd changed her. That once-despised name no longer sounded like a snide jibe. Instead, it sounded like a vow of lifelong fealty.

"No, it's even better than that, *mo chridhe.*" She summoned a tremulous smile and cupped his jaw in one shaking hand. "I'm now Ellen, lady to William Mackinnon of Achnasheen, my lord and my love."

She saw how her fervent declaration moved him to the soul. As Will bent his head and kissed her, Ellen knew that this man's love was all the freedom she'd ever need.

EPILOGUE

Achnasheen, Western Highlands of Scotland, September 1733

"There's never been a more beautiful bairn since the world began," Will said with soft emphasis, as he stared down at his newborn son, who slept in his arms after a squalling entrance into the world.

Ellen's smile was weary, as she rested against a pile of pillows. She turned toward the armchair beside the bed. It contained the new arrival and her handsome husband of a year. "Och, beloved, you're biased."

Jean, Achnasheen's healer and midwife, gave an indulgent snicker from where she stood beside the sideboard, sorting through a mysterious array of vials and bottles and packets. "My lady, he is a beautiful bairn. The image of Master William when he was born."

It was late. After a labor that had extended through most of the day, Ellen was exhausted. Exhausted, but happy.

“Thank ye, my darling.” Will raised his head from admiring the baby. “He’s perfect.”

She loved the glow in his eyes. He’d turned out to be a loving husband. Now it seemed that he’d be a loving father. Not that she’d ever doubted it.

“I willnae argue.” Ellen held out her hand and Will caught it, bringing it to his lips for a fervent kiss.

He smiled, as if she made the sun rise every day. "And you're perfect."

“I willnae argue with that either.” Once she might have looked for a sneer hidden in the extravagant compliment. No longer. Marriage to Will had shown her that perfection came in many different guises, including in the form of a woman with one leg shorter than the other.

Even that wasn’t as bad as it used to be. Jean’s skill and care over the last year had made an enormous difference to Ellen’s ease of movement. She was never likely to win a sprint race or climb Ben Nevis, but she had no trouble managing the stairs here at Achnasheen or at Glen Aric, the pretty estate about twenty miles away, where she and Will had settled after their marriage. She even made a fair job of dancing at family celebrations. With Will’s help.

Jean’s expertise had brought Ellen to Achnasheen to have her first child. That, and Will’s wish to see the next generation born at the clan chieftain’s seat. Ellen studied the baby cuddled in her husband’s powerful arms and tried to imagine that one day he would be lord of the mighty Mackinnons.

Right now, that required more imagination than she possessed. A thought which amused her. When her book had been published in July, the critics had tumbled over themselves praising the rich prose and vivid imagination that she'd used to retell the old legends.

A soft knock announced the arrival of the current mighty chieftain of the clan. And his equally powerful lady.

That was another reason Ellen was at Achnasheen for the birth. Over the last year, she'd come to love Will's parents. They'd welcomed her with a wholehearted generosity that provided a cruel contrast with her own father's callous treatment. They also offered an example of enduring love that she hoped and prayed she and Will would emulate. Seeing Callum and Mhairi together, it was hard to believe that their union had begun in violent warfare between feuding families. It was clear that in this clan, dramatic beginnings to good marriages were the rule.

Ellen spared a fleeting thought for her father, sulking on Inchgallen. She'd written to tell him of her marriage, but had received no reply. He'd once rejected her for her lameness. Now it seemed that he rejected her because she'd defied him and run off to wed. Likely he also resented the ignominious role that he played in the ballads that spread across the Highlands, telling of how gallant William Mackinnon had eloped with Fair Ellen of the Isles.

"We ken it's late, but we'd love to see the wean," Mhairi said from the doorway. As a girl, she'd been a famous beauty. Now contentment lent her a radiance that belied her more than fifty years. "Do ye mind if we come in?"

"No' at all. I was about to ask Will to send for ye," Ellen said, smiling with genuine pleasure.

Mhairi and Callum stepped forward, hand in hand. Callum was still tall and strong, although the mane of black hair that had inspired the nickname

Black Callum was now streaked with silver. He smiled at Ellen. "How are ye feeling?"

She glanced across at Mhairi, who had assisted Jean at the birth. A silent shared moment, as both recalled the day's difficulties. It hadn't been an easy delivery, but worth it in the end. "Like a proud mother."

As Jean slipped out of the room, Will stood and carried the baby across to his parents. "Mamma and Da, may I present my son, Callum Cameron Mackinnon?"

Ellen's smile broadened, as surprised delight flooded her father-in-law's hawkish face. Will's coloring came from his mother, but the sculpted bone structure and aristocratic manner were all his sire's. "Och, ye called him Callum?"

As Will passed the boy into his grandmother's arms, he looked rather emotional himself. "Aye. Ellen and I decided to name him after the finest man we know. That's ye, Da."

"Well, I'm...I'm speechless, that's what I am." He peered over Mhairi's shoulder at the stirring infant. "I must say he's much more beautiful than his namesake."

Mhairi bestowed a fond smile on her husband. "Ye have your moments, *mo chridhe*."

Will laughed and returned to sit beside Ellen on the bed. For the moment, his parents' attention was all on the younger Callum, so he took the opportunity to kiss her. "Thank you, my darling. I love ye more than I can say. I bless the day my boat bumped into Bortha and I discovered my destiny."

"I love ye, too, Will," she murmured, kissing him back with all the joy that filled her heart.

ABOUT THE AUTHOR

Australian Anna Campbell has written 11 multi award-winning historical romances for Avon HarperCollins and Grand Central Publishing. As an independently published author, she's released more than 30 bestselling stories. Right now, she is working on a new series called A Scandal in Mayfair, set amidst the glamour and sensuality of Regency London. Anna has won numerous awards for her stories, including RT Book Reviews Reviewers Choice, the Booksellers Best, the Golden Quill (three times), the Heart of Excellence (twice), the Write Touch, the Aspen Gold (twice), and the Australian Romance Readers' favorite historical romance (five times).

Anna loves to hear from her readers. You can find her at:

Website: www.annacampbell.com

facebook.com/AnnaCampbellFans

twitter.comAnnaCampbellOz

bookbub.com/authors/anna-campbell

The Laird's Willful Lass: The Lairds Most Likely Book 1

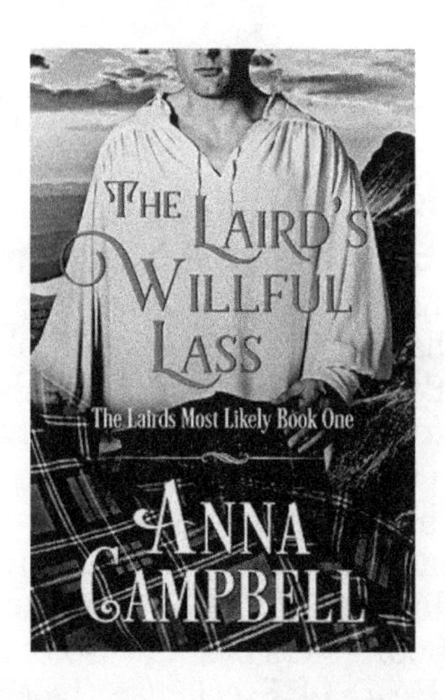

An untamed man as immovable as a Highland mountain...

Fergus Mackinnon, autocratic Laird of Achnasheen, likes to be in charge. When he was little more than a lad, he became master of his Scottish estate, and he's learned to rely on his unfailing judgment. So has everyone else in his corner of the world. He sees no reason for his bride—when he finds her—to be any different.

A headstrong woman from the warm and passionate south...

Marina Lucchetti knows all about fighting her way through a wall of masculine arrogance. In her native Florence, she's become a successful artist, no easy feat for a woman. Now a commission to paint a series of Highland scenes promises to spread her fame far and wide. When a carriage accident strands her at Achnasheen for a few weeks, it's a mixed blessing. The magnificent landscape offers everything her artistic soul could desire. If only she can resist the impulse to smash her easel across the laird's obstinate head.

When two fiery souls come together, a conflagration flares.

Marina is Fergus's worst nightmare—a woman who defies a man's guidance. Fergus challenges everything Marina believes about a woman's right to choose her path. No two people could be less suited. But when irresistible passion enters the equation, good sense soon jumps into the loch.

Will the desire between Fergus and Marina blaze hot, then fade to ashes? Or will the imperious laird and his willful lass discover that their differences aren't insurmountable after all, but the spice that will flavor a lifetime of happiness?

The Laird's Christmas Kiss: The Lairds Most Likely Book 2

Down with love!

Ever since she was fifteen, shy wallflower Elspeth Douglas has pined in vain for the attentions of dashing Brody Girvan, Laird of Invermackie. But the rakish Highlander doesn't even know she's alive. Now she's twenty, she realizes that she'll never be happy until she stops loving her brother's handsome friend. When family and friends gather at Achnasheen Castle for Christmas, she intends to show the world that she's all grown up, and grown out of silly crushes on gorgeous Scotsmen. So take that, my gallant laddie!

Girls just want to have fun...

Except it turns out that Brody isn't singing from the same Christmas carol sheet. Elspeth decides she's not interested in him anymore, just as he decides he's very interested indeed. In fact, now he looks more closely, his friend Hamish's sister is pretty and funny and forthright – and just the lassie to share his Highland estate. Convincing his little wren of his romantic intentions is difficult enough, even before she undergoes a makeover and becomes the belle of Achnasheen. For once in his life, dissolute Brody is burdened with honorable intentions, while the lady he pursues is set on flirtation with no strings attached.

Deck the halls with mistletoe!

With interfering friends and a crate of imported mistletoe thrown into the mix, the stage is set for a house party rife with secrets, clandestine kisses, misunderstandings, heartache, scandal, and love triumphant.

The Highlander's Lost Lady: The Lairds Most Likely Book 3

A Highlander as brave and strong as a knight of old...

When Diarmid Mactavish, Laird of Invertavey, discovers a mysterious woman washed up on his land after a wild storm, he takes her in and tries to find her family. But even as forbidden dreams of sensual fulfillment torment him, he's convinced that this beautiful lassie isn't what she seems. And if there's one thing Diarmid despises, it's a liar.

A mother willing to do anything to save her daughter...

Widow Fiona Grant has risked everything to break free of her clan and rescue her adolescent daughter from a forced marriage. But before her quest has barely begun, disaster strikes. She escapes her brutish kinsmen, only to be shipwrecked on Mactavish territory where she falls into her enemies' hands. For centuries, a murderous feud has raged between the Mactavishes and the Grants, so how can she trust her darkly handsome host?

Now a twisted Highland road leads to danger and passion...and irresistible love. But is love strong enough to banish the past's long shadows and offer these wary allies all that their hearts desire?

The Highlander's Defiant Captive: The Lairds Most Likely Book 4

Peace in the glens means war in the bedchamber!

Scotland. 1699. In a time of heroes, the greatest hero of all is Callum Mackinnon, Laird of Achnasheen. Brave, reckless, canny, and handsome enough to turn any lassie weak at the knees, Callum is a legend in the wild corner of the Highlands where he rules. Now the young laird is determined to choose a new path for his clan and end the violent feud with the Drummonds, a conflict that has painted the glens red with blood for centuries. This means taking Bonny Mhairi Drummond, the Rose of Bruard, as his wife. When negotiations with her pig-headed father break down, Callum seizes matters into his own hands and kidnaps the fairest maiden in Scotland, swearing to make her his own.

Bonny Mhairi is the adored only child of Clan

Drummond's doughty chieftain and she's inherited all her father's courage and stubbornness. Not to mention his undying hatred for anyone called Mackinnon. When the Mackinnon chieftain steals her away from her home and vows to woo her into accepting him as her husband, she swears that she'll never consent to be his bride. But trapped inside her foe's castle, Mhairi finds it hard to cling to old certainties. She detests her arrogant jailer, even as he sparks a fierce, forbidden hunger in her soul.

Loving the enemy...

As Callum and Mhairi wage their passionate war of hearts, danger, treachery and desire circle closer and closer. When her father's army masses at the gates of Achnasheen, will Mhairi prove herself a Drummond now and forever? Or will new allegiances trump ancient hatred, as the desperate laird battles to win the lass he loves more than his life?

The Highlander's Christmas Quest: The Lairds Most Likely Book 5

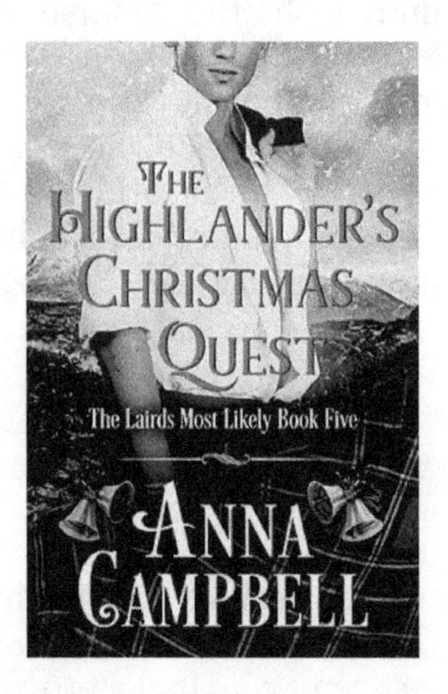

She's found the man for her, but he has no plans to stay on her island. Perhaps it's time to try a little sabotage!

Scotland. 1725. The moment she sees handsome Dougal Drummond, Kirsty Macbain tumbles headlong into love. A chance storm a few days before Christmas has blown the gallant Highlander off-course to her father's isle of Askaval, but once he's repaired his boat, Dougal is determined to continue on his way. His bright blue eyes are firmly fixed on valiant deeds and a distant horizon. What does he care for a smart-mouthed, independent lassie who forms no part of his plans for his future?

Kirsty is convinced that if only she can keep Dougal on Askaval, he'll see how perfect they are together. With his boat out of action, he's trapped in her company. Some surreptitious midnight destruction with a drill and a hammer might help true love to win out. On the other hand, if Dougal discovers what she's been up to, there will be the devil to pay.

Will this madcap Christmas deliver Kirsty's heart's desire – or will her scheming see Dougal sailing away to a life without her?

The Highlander's English Bride: The Lairds Most Likely Book 6

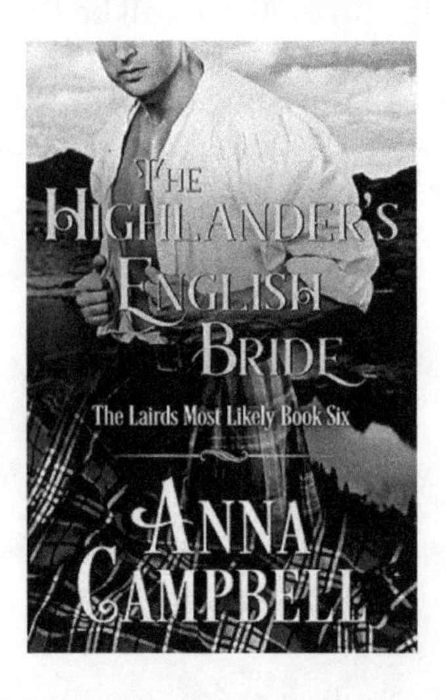

An impossible pairing...

Hamish Douglas, the mercurial Laird of Glen Lyon, has never got along with independent, smart-mouthed Emily Baylor. Which wouldn't matter if this brilliant Scottish astronomer didn't move in the same scientific circles as Emily and if her famous father wasn't his mentor. But when Emily looks likely to derail the event which will make Hamish's career, he loses his temper with the pretty miss and his recklessness leaves her reputation in ruins.

A marriage made in scandal...

Emily has always thought her father's spectacular protégé was far too arrogant for his own good. But what is she to do when the only way she can save her good name in society is to wed the unruly laird? Reluctantly she accepts Hamish's proposal, but only on the condition that their union remains chaste. That shouldn't be a problem; they've never been friends, let alone potential lovers – except that after they marry, Hamish reveals unexpected depths and a host of admirable qualities, and he's so awfully handsome, and now the swaggering rogue admits that he desires her...

From the ballrooms of London to the grandeur of the western Highlands, a battle royal rages between these two strong-willed combatants. Neither plans to yield an inch – but are these smart people smart enough to see that sometimes the greatest victory lies in mutual surrender?

The Highlander's Forbidden Mistress: The Lairds Most Likely Book 7

A week to be wicked...

Widowed Selina Martin faces another marriage founded on duty, not love. When notorious libertine Lord Bruard invites her to his isolated hunting lodge, he promises discretion – and seven days of hedonistic pleasure before she weds her boorish fiancé. All her life, Selina has done the right thing, but this no-strings-attached chance to discover the handsome rake's sensual secrets is irresistible. She'll surrender to her wicked fantasies, seize some brief happiness, then knuckle down to a loveless union. What could possibly go wrong?

In a lifetime of seduction, Brock Drummond, the dashing Earl of Bruard, has never wanted a woman the way he wants demure widow Selina Martin. When Selina agrees to become his temporary lover, he soon falls captive to an enchantment unlike any other. He sets out to slake his white hot desire until only ashes remain, but as each day of forbidden delight passes, the idea of saying goodbye to his ardent mistress becomes more and more unbearable.

When scandal explodes around them and threatens to destroy Selina, Brock is the only person she can turn to. After so short a time, can she trust a man whose name is a byword for depravity?

Will this sizzling liaison prove a mere affair to remember? Or will their week of passion spark a lifetime of happiness for the widow and her dissolute Scottish earl?

The Highlander's Christmas Countess: The Lairds Most Likely Book 8

The new stableboy has a secret!

Kit Laing is a genius with Glen Lyon's horses and a favorite with his employer's family, but he isn't all he seems. In fact, the shy stablehand isn't a he at all. Kit is actually Christabel Urquhart, Countess of Appin, on the run from a greedy, violent stepbrother with designs on her fortune.

And the laird's handsome nephew has worked out just what it is.

Quentin MacNab, the dashing heir to Cannich, has had his suspicions about the new stable lad from the first. Kit is far too pretty to be a boy – and far too well spoken to be a servant.

Now passion and danger combine to create a Yuletide like no other.

When a snowstorm traps Kit and Quentin overnight in an isolated hut, the discovery of her true identity sparks a rushed marriage to stave off a scandal. But can the Christmas Countess learn to trust her charming new husband's promises of protection? Or will their fragile alliance fall victim to the evil forces assailing her?

The Highlander's Rescued Maiden: The Lairds Most Likely Book 9

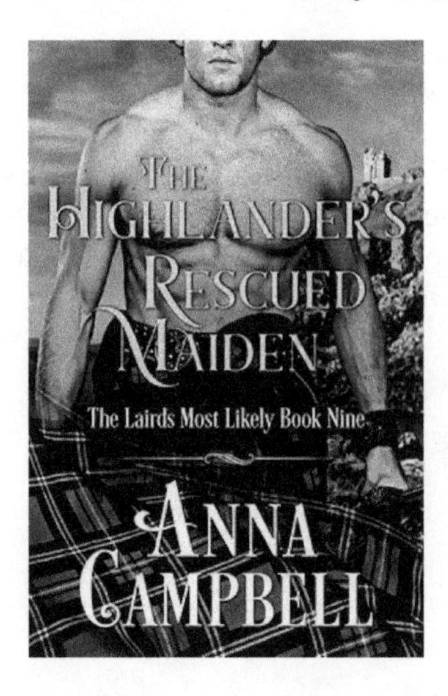

The myth of Fair Ellen of the Isles.

Across the Highlands, people recount the legend of a beautiful lassie in a tower, locked away from her clamorous suitors by a tyrannical father. Any person of sense dismisses the story as a fairy tale, no more substantial than a wisp of Scottish mist.

Rogue or hero? Or a little bit of both?

Dashing Highlander Will Mackinnon is a devil with the ladies, disinclined to fall for such romantic nonsense. But one day, his storm-tossed boat washes ashore at a rocky island dominated by a stone tower. Inside the tower, he discovers lovely, gallant Ellen Cameron and a passion that eclipses anything he's experienced before in his reckless life.

Danger and desire...

This brave adventurer vows to rescue the captive maiden and make her his own forever. But dark shadows gather about the lovers and threaten to destroy all their hopes for happiness. Will has found the love of a lifetime – but will it end up costing him his life?

The Highlander's Christmas Lassie: The Lairds Most Likely Book 10

Young love torn apart.

As teenagers, Malcolm Innes and Rhona Macleod fell passionately in love. But Malcom's parents were horrified to think of the aristocratic heir to Dun Carron marrying a humble crofter's daughter. Desperate to crush the affair, they locked Malcolm up and exiled Rhona to London where she disappears. But Malcolm is faithful and stubborn and devotes his life to searching for his beloved and the child she was carrying when they were cruelly separated.

A chance to mend two shattered lives.

On a snowy Christmas Eve, Rhona opens the door of her isolated farmhouse to find the man she never thought to see again, the man who betrayed her. When she was pregnant with his son, Malcolm abandoned her to find her way alone in a cold, heartless world. Now she discovers that her long-held hatred is based on lies and that he's been true to her. Yet surely after all these years, it's too late to awaken the love that once united them.

As Christmas Eve turns into Christmas Day, Malcolm and Rhona discover that their mutual desire has never died. Will this Yuletide reunion lead to a lifetime together? Or has old tragedy ruptured their bond forever?

CPSIA information can be obtained
at www.ICGtesting.com
Printed in the USA
LVHW100831160722
723665LV00004B/115